Lucas and Lionel

First Edition

Published by The Nazca Plains Corporation
Las Vegas, Nevada
2010

ISBN: 978-1-935509-84-4

Published by

The Nazca Plains Corporation ®
4640 Paradise Rd, Suite 141
Las Vegas NV 89109-8000

PUBLISHER'S NOTE
Lucas and Lionel is a work of fiction created wholly by *LT Ville*'s
imagination. All characters are fictional and any resemblance to
any persons living or deceased is purely by accident. No portion of
this book reflects any real person or events.

Cover Images
Thomas Pullicino,
Tom Fullum Photography,
Tono Balaguer

Art Director
Blake Stephens

Lucas and Lionel

First Edition

LT Ville

Contents

Contents continued...

Chapter 1

The Incident

My freshman year of college turned out to be more interesting than I expected. I was an average looking white guy. I was 5'11" with brown hair and brown eyes and a naturally skinny body. I didn't have muscles, but if I really focused and flexed my arms as hard as I could, small biceps and triceps appeared.

I was a star guard on my high school basketball team. I spent most of my free time hanging out with my basketball teammates. I particularly loved hanging out with Lionel.

Lionel was and still is a fine ass black guy. His skin was a silky smooth chocolate canvas that I wanted to paint all over, if you catch my drift. He was 6'2" and his body was much better than mine. He had an eight pack for goodness sake. He didn't have to flex to make a muscle because his body was well toned and his muscles were well defined. I loved that he wasn't bulky though. I had a thing against bodybuilder types. Oh, and his dick. All I could say was, "Wow!" I had seen his dick a million times over the past few years and he lived up to the stereotype. His dick must have been about 9 inches when it was soft, and it was thick too. Sometimes I wondered if my small self could handle him, but truthfully, I didn't care. If he ever decided to dish it out, I would do whatever I had to do to take it.

Lionel's first name was Jay, but I couldn't break the habit of calling him Lionel. Plus I thought Lucas and Lionel sounded cuter than Lucas and Jay. I wasn't the only person who called him Lionel though. He had to go by Lionel on the basketball team because there was already another Jay and there were about four other guys on the team with the same last name as him. Coach didn't want confusion when he yelled out names, so Lionel told him it was okay to call him Lionel.

How Lionel became my college roommate was interesting. I didn't know he was planning on going to my school. He had basketball scholarships to schools all over the country, but he never made an official announcement about where he was going. I assumed he was going to stay close to home. I asked him about it a few times and he said he hadn't made a decision. He was gone all summer, playing basketball in a summer league. I talked to him on the phone once or twice, but I assumed I would never see him again.

Anyway, my dorm door had two names on it. One was Lucas; the other was Lionel. I almost passed out, but I knew it couldn't be my Lionel. He would have told me something like that. I unlocked the door and there he was, sitting at one of the computer desks, playing a game on his laptop.

He paused his game and turned around, "What's up Lucas?" He stood. "Oh and you brought the fam too! How you doing Mr. and Mrs. Donnelly?" He was grinning from ear to ear. My parents said hello to him, and I smiled. I was speechless. I sat my orientation package on one of the beds and noticed that he hadn't picked a bed. Lionel walked to me, "I haven't seen you since graduation night! Boy you better give me some love!" He opened his arms and I fell in to them with no questions asked.

I put my arms around him and pulled him closer. I said, "I missed you man!" Then I pushed back a little and said, "You don't call! You don't write! And now you pop up here?" I tried to say it jokingly.

He took it as a joke and laughed. Then he moved his arms from around me and threw his arms in the air, "Surprise!" His entire face lit up when he said that.

My hands were resting on his hips. I didn't want to let go, but I knew I had to, so I moved my hands and started a conversation about something else. "When did you get here?"

"This morning."

"Why didn't you pick a bed?"

"Well, it doesn't matter to me where I sleep. I was waiting for you to get here so you could pick. I'll sleep in the one that's left over."

"Did you know I was the Lucas that would be living here?"

"Of course! I requested you as my roommate!"

I blushed. I couldn't help it. A warm sensation ran through my veins and stopped when it reached my cheeks. Then, to make the matter worse, my mother said, "Aw, you made him blush!" Talk about embarrassing! I wanted to disappear.

My parents knew I was gay. My father wasn't very accepting, but he tolerated me because I was his son. My mother however, was extremely accepting. She joined the local chapter of PFLAG. She looked up tons of information and I never doubted for a second that my mother loved me unconditionally. She wanted me to tell everyone, but I wasn't ready for that step. My father was grateful that I wasn't ready, because for all intents and purposes, I was still the same son he had grown to love. He and I enjoyed pretending I wasn't gay. It made life easier for both of us.

To make a long story only moderately long, Lionel and I were roommates. We were about halfway through our first semester and he had no idea I was gay. I had gotten in to the gay scene in a nearby town, so I had a lot of gay friends, but Lionel hadn't met any of them. I had also gotten in to the bad habit of bringing a guy home with me on the nights when I knew Lionel would be gone. It was always the same guy: Michael.

I lost my virginity to Michael in my dorm room. I met him at a club and he was cute. We hit it off right away and we both had a little too much to drink. He wanted to see my dorm room, and I wanted company because I knew Lionel was gone for the night. We went back to my room and turned on the television. He leaned over and started kissing me. To my surprise, I kissed him back. It wasn't like I had never kissed a guy. I kissed plenty of boys when I was younger and experimenting, but none of them counted as real kisses because all those idiots turned out to be straight!

Michael started touching me and everything he did felt good. He was definitely experienced. The next thing I knew, we were naked and in a 69 position sucking each other. I had never sucked a dick.

I hoped I was doing a good job, but I couldn't tell. I tried to suck in as much of his 7 inches as I could. I didn't know what to do with my hands, so I wrapped my arms around his waist and massaged his butt with my hands. His butt was nice and soft, but I was more interested in his dick.

I felt a finger tracing a path up and down my crack. His oral manipulations, coupled with his finger, were driving me wild. His finger started applying pressure to my hole. I tried to be still. His finger slipped in and it felt incredible. He pulled his finger out and took my dick out of his mouth. "Get on all fours." I followed his command like he was a drill sergeant. I released his dick from my mouth and got on all fours. Within seconds his tongue was assaulting my ass with such finesse and vigor that all I could do was moan my appreciation. He inserted his finger in my ass again and started pumping the finger in and out. He inserted two, then three. He took out his fingers and asked, "You ready?"

Fear hit me. I felt the alcohol escaping my body, and my sanity immediately returned. "I'm a virgin!" I shouted.

"I'll be gentle."

Somehow that soothed me and made it okay again. "Do you have a condom?"

"Of course."

"Okay, let's do it then." I rationalized that I could always blame it on the alcohol when it was over.

"Do you have any lube or something?"

"Top drawer."

I heard him reach over and open the drawer. He took out my lube, which came in handy for self pleasuring. He must have gotten a lot on his finger because his finger felt cool as it entered my ass again. He rubbed the lube around inside me. Then I heard him open a condom and I wondered where the condom came from. He put the condom on, and soon I felt his dick pushing against my hole. "You sure you're ready?"

"Yes."

"Okay, I'm going to go slow at first, so just relax and try to push out like you're taking a shit."

That wasn't exactly the image I wanted to have in my mind at a moment like that, but his advice made his slow entrance tolerable. Once he was all the way in, he rested for a moment. It felt strange feeling his balls and pubic hair resting on my butt, yet feeling his dick inside me seemed normal.

He was good at sex. He started going in and out, slowly. Then he picked up the pace and added a slight swaying move that resulted in his dick hitting that special place inside me. My orgasm set off his orgasm and we both collapsed on the bed. I fell asleep in his arms.

The next morning, I woke up to an empty bed and instantly panicked. I couldn't believe my first time had been so tawdry and I was about to cry when my door opened. Michael walked in wearing a pair of boxers.

"I had to use the bathroom."

"It's okay!"

"So, um. Will I see you again?"

I couldn't believe he was asking me that. I should have been the one saying that to him. "If you want to."

"Well I definitely want to." He smiled at me and walked over to place a sweet kiss on my lips.

We talked for most of the morning. I told him I was in love with Lionel and he said it was okay, because he wasn't looking for anything too serious. He said I seemed like a cool person, and suggested we keep it casual.

Eventually, he had to go to work. We exchanged numbers and he left. I took my shower at 3.

Lionel was supposed to be back around 7, so I was beginning to worry when 8 pm rolled around and he was still gone. He called me at 8:10 to let me know that he would be gone for the night again. I wondered what he was doing.

Everything caught up with me about a month later. I was on my bed with Michael plowing away at my ass. We were playing our role play game again. I was calling him Lionel and moaning his name. Michael seemed to get off on pretending to be Lionel. We had the music turned on to muffle the sounds, so no one walking by would hear anything. I was about to cum, so I started getting a little louder, "Oh, Lionel. Oh, oh, oh!"

"What the fuck!"

I looked over and saw Lionel standing there with the door open. He looked at me. His eyes had a strange look in them. I watched, speechless, as the door began to close and he disappeared from sight.

Chapter 2

Tracing the Surface

The next few days were torture. I hadn't seen Lionel since the incident and I was fairly certain that he left campus. I called his cell all night after he caught me, but Michael told me to give Lionel some space, so I hadn't tried to call him since. I wished I could talk to Lionel. I had been waiting for him to walk through the door. I had eaten very little food. I only showered once, right after the incident. I tried to rush when I used the bathroom because I was afraid he would come back and grab some of his things, and I would miss him. I wouldn't let Michael, or anyone else come over, because I didn't want Lionel to return and find someone else in the room with me. I wanted Lionel to walk in and have no excuse not to talk to me.

Knowing Lionel was out there somewhere, harboring my secret, was nerve wrecking because I didn't know if he had told anyone. What if Lionel said something to one of the other guys on the team? I loved basketball almost as much as I loved Lionel. I couldn't believe I had made such a mess of my life in such little time. I never expected I would one day star in my own soap opera.

It was Monday night and Lionel had been gone since Friday evening. I was really worried about him. I skipped all my classes that day so I could stay in my room and wait for him. I had no idea if he went to any of his classes. If he did, he went without his books and his notebooks. My mother called because she was worried. She hadn't heard from me all weekend and she knew something was wrong. I told her Lionel found out I was gay. She asked how he found out. I told her he walked in on me kissing another guy. She asked when it happened. I said Friday night and she got upset. She started yelling at me for not calling her sooner. She complained because I didn't come to her in my time of crisis and she reminded me that she was my mother and she could handle any situation. I was tempted to tell her the truth was I was getting fucked up the ass when Lionel walked in. I figured that would test her tolerance, but I wanted to maintain some of my dignity and telling my mom about my sex life would only serve to make me feel worse.

I was about to tell her I had to go when I heard a key in the lock. My mother was talking about something, but I completely ignored her as I stared at the door. I swear the door opened in slow motion. Lionel walked in and closed the door. He was wearing the same clothes he had on when he left and I couldn't help but wonder if he had showered. What used to be a shadow on his face was a light trace of a beard. He looked at me and I saw the saddest look I had ever seen in my life.

I quickly said goodbye to my mother, "Mom, I gotta go." I hung up the phone and waited for a sign from Lionel. Lionel stared at me a few minutes longer. I began to feel uncomfortable with the silence and I prepared to say something. It was the speech I had been practicing for the last three days. Lionel walked to his bed and sat, never taking his eyes off of me.

"So how long have you known that you were gay?" Gone was the sweet, jovial ring that I used to hear in his voice. All that was left behind was the sound of sadness.

"For a long time, but I didn't accept it until our sophomore year." I wanted to be as honest and as direct as I could be.

"So you knew all of high school?"

"Yes."

"What made you that way?" I was flabbergasted by the question, but the look of sincerity in his eyes told me he wasn't trying to be offensive.

"I was born this way."

"Oh." He looked lost in thought.

"Your mother wants you to call her." I had so many things planned to say to him, and when I finally got my chance, I couldn't find the words. All I could do was relay a stupid message.

He seemed to snap back to reality. "I already talked to her."

"Oh."

"So your friend's name is Lionel, too?"

"No, it's Michael." I immediately recognized my mistake. I shouldn't have said that. I knew what the next question was going to be.

"So why were you calling him Lionel?"

"I don't know." I started to fidget on my bed.

"Oh." He looked down at the floor and returned to his thoughts.

I watched him try to burn a hole in the floor with his eyes. He stared at the same spot for so long that I took a glance to make sure there wasn't anything there. I wondered what thoughts were bouncing around in that sexy head of his. Then I verbally bashed myself for thinking his head was sexy at a time like that. I finally couldn't take it anymore, so I spoke.

"Did you tell anyone about me?"

He looked up and I realized I had hurt his feelings. The question was necessary, but the look of hurt in his eyes made me feel like less of a person for even thinking to ask such a thing.

"Of course I didn't! What type of a guy do you think I am?"

"I don't know."

I heard him mumble under his breath, "Yeah, that's right, you don't know."

"Huh? What did you say?" I heard what he said, but I wanted him to repeat it.

"Nothing."

"No, you said something." I had no idea why I was pressing him to repeat it.

"I said you don't know. I was going to say you don't know, but you should know, but I thought I should keep that to myself."

I decided it was best for me to move on with the conversation, "So how do you feel about this whole situation?"

"Well, I'm surprised. I never would have guessed you liked boys. I want to say I'm okay with it, but I'm not sure where I am on that issue. All I know is that you're my boy and we can work this out." He stood and walked over to me.

I was shocked because his reaction seemed unrealistic. "Why are you being so accepting?"

"Three nights sleeping on the ground really puts things in to perspective. I'm lucky to have a roof over my head. I'm lucky that you've always been a good friend to me. I'm lucky that we won't have the drama of fighting over some chick." He smiled, and I saw a hint of hope in his eyes. I happily smiled with him. "Now give me a hug." He opened his arms.

I stood and surrendered to his warm embrace. The sheer joy from his acceptance, or at least tolerance of me overwhelmed my senses. I started crying and shaking in his arms. He pulled me closer and softly said, "Ssh. It'll be okay." He rubbed my back with his hands, creating heat and setting my skin on fire. I buried my face in his t-shirt. It was then that I realized the weird smell that came in with him was not from his shoes. He stunk!

I let him know in no uncertain times that he needed to clean up, by taking a big whiff of air, and saying, "Phew! You need a shower! You stink!" I leaned back wiping my tears away with the back of my hands.

"Well you don't smell like a bed of roses either." His comment made me laugh, and my eyes started leaking tears of laughter and joy. I knew it wasn't that funny, but I couldn't stop laughing. Lionel joined me. We stood like that for a while, me lost in his warm embrace, and both of us laughing hysterically. Whoever said laughter was good for the soul was right on the money. We laughed until we couldn't laugh and then we joked about it and laughed some more. I watched as the traces of sadness began to vacate his eyes, and the happy spirit I knew and loved returned. We weren't whole again, but we were on the right track.

Chapter 3

Not a Word

The next week was tolerable. Lionel and I talked a lot but the incident became the elephant in the room. We didn't talk about it, but I thought we both needed it that way. I was scared that rubbing his nose in who I was would push him away and that was the last thing I wanted to do. I had talked to my mother a few times since Lionel and I made up and she was still bitter because I didn't tell her what was going on right away. Sometimes she could be really needy. She was so afraid of being a bad mother, or having me lose touch with her, that she failed to distinguish between my personal business and her motherly rights. I didn't understand why she was so desperate to be needed. I knew my father needed her enough for both of us.

I had so much work to do that week. I had a paper due in two of my classes, I had started a work study job, and as if that wasn't enough, I worked out in the mornings with Lionel. We usually went for a morning run then hit the gym to lift weights. I tended to play around in the weight room, but Lionel was always serious and made sure he got a good workout. I kept telling Lionel we didn't need to work out before the first practice. We had never done that in high school. Back then, we played pick-up games year round so we were always ready to go. College was different though. I didn't hang out with the same type of crowd. Lionel, however, was surrounded by basketball types and seemed to always be talking about some pick-up game he played. It was no longer us; it was Lionel, and it was Lucas. We had both made adjustments to college. I just wished we had made them together.

I had talked to Michael everyday that week. He had been such a good friend to me and his advice had been good as well. I thought I would have driven myself crazy if he wasn't around to keep me sane. I wanted to tell him he was my best friend, but I didn't want to hurt his feelings. Calling him my best friend was as good as castrating him. At least that was how he would see it. He had issues of his own to work through, mostly with friendships gone awry. Things and people were so much simpler in high school. But I wouldn't go back there to save my life.

Lionel walked in the room wearing only a towel and my attention was immediately focused on him. I tried not to stare. I pretended to read my book, but I kept glancing up as he walked between his bed and his closet. He was looking for something to wear and depressing me at the same time. Watching him walk back and forth made me feel sad because I knew I would never have him the way I wanted him. I was in the process of studying his back with my eyes and appreciating the nice contrast between the white towel and his chocolate skin. His butt looked perfect in his towel. I wanted to walk over and grab his ass, but I knew that was the worst thing I could do. He moved to turn around and I looked at my book.

"Yo Lucas." I looked up at him standing there with his upper body exposed. I had to remind myself to keep looking up. I found his eyes and tried to keep my gaze above his neck. He hadn't pranced around half naked since the incident, but there he was, basically parading his body for me to see. He had to know he was eye candy. The thought of how badly I wanted him, made me sad. I looked away from Lionel and glanced towards the door. I hoped he hadn't noticed the look in my eyes. "Lucas!" I looked at him without thinking. He noticed my expression and I could see the question developing in his head. "What's wrong?"

"Nothing." My voice was shaky.

"You sure?"

"Yeah, man. This book just reminded me of something." I knew it was a bad lie the second the words left my lips.

"Really? Is math that bad?" He gave a half laugh.

Shit. I was an idiot. I was sitting there with my nose buried in a math book talking about the book reminded me of something. "I was just thinking that I might actually fail Calculus II. I don't know what possessed me to sign up for it." I felt a tear drop and I didn't know what to say, so I babbled, "If I fail, I won't be on the basketball team, and I'd rather die." I knew that wasn't true. My other grades would easily cover up an F, plus I was doing okay in math. I would at least get a B. I was having a meltdown, wondering what he thought of me, and constantly reminding myself that there was no hope for us. I was talking about math, but my tears were for him, for us.

He came over to me and pulled me in to a hug. I dropped the book and hugged him back. My nose was crushed against his chest and the tears began to fall even faster. "Relax man, you won't fail math, and even if you do, you'll still be on the team." His voice sounded fatherly as he tried to soothe me. I wasn't thinking about his voice though. I was distracted by the feel of his bare flesh under my hands. I rubbed my hands up and down his back a few times before I stopped myself. I turned my face to the side so that my ear was pressed firmly against his chest. I could hear his heart beating, but all I was thinking about was how good he smelled. I wanted to stick out my tongue and lick his beautiful skin, but I would never do that.

"I can't do this," I said. "I've made a mess of everything."

"Just relax. Everything will be okay." I wanted to yell at him. I wanted to tell him nothing would ever be okay again. I wanted to tell him that he wasn't the one secretly in love with his roommate. There were so many things I wanted to say, but only my sniffles could be heard. "Come on man. Stop that! You can get a tutor and everything will be fine." He lifted one of his hands and rubbed it through my hair. "Come on. Get a grip." I thought, 'I love you. How's that for a grip?' Suddenly, I heard Lionel speaking in a playful and almost devilish voice, "I know what will make you stop crying." He started tickling me and I couldn't help but laugh. I crumpled down on my bed and tried to use my arms to protect myself, but his assault was relentless. I didn't stop laughing until his fingers stopped attacking my body. I felt much better, and not because Lionel was touching me and playing with me, but because I finally had a good cry. My mother always told me nothing lifted the spirit from the dumps like a good cry. Each tear was a small piece of the pain falling.

I realized I had been sitting there for a few seconds, so I looked up and unexpectedly made eye contact with Lionel. The look in his eyes told me he was waiting for me to say something. I wiped my tear-stained face on my shirt. "Sorry about that. I guess I was having a gay moment." I wanted to shoot myself the second the sentence was floated out in to the air for him to hear.

To my surprise, he smiled and said, "Yeah, I guess you were." He walked back to his bed and picked up two jerseys. He turned around and held them up for me to see. "Now which one should I wear tonight?"

I wanted to say, 'Gee thanks for caring. I have an emotional meltdown and you ask me which shirt you should wear.' But all I said was, "The white one, it looks nice with your complexion." I grabbed my dick through my shorts as I said it, and gave it a good squeeze. I was hoping to relieve some tension between us. It was something I would have done without question two weeks before.

Lionel's smile got wider. "Fuck you!" That was the response I was looking for. He reached to grab his package through the towel to return the gesture, but his towel fell. His gorgeous body was a flash of brown as he bent down quickly to pick up the towel and put it back around his waist. I wished I could have seen something, but maybe next time.

"So where are you off to this evening?"

"Hot date."

"Oh. Do I know her?"

"Probably not."

"Oh." I picked up my math book and tried to find the next lesson. I wanted to appear busy. Lionel put on his clothes and I sat on my bed pretending to work. The silence wasn't broken until twenty minutes later when he said goodbye.

I was left in my room, alone as usual, with nothing but time to think. I called Michael and told him about my meltdown. He tried to tell me it was okay, but we both knew it wasn't. After a few minutes of talking, I decided to go over to his place. I packed a few things and left a note for Lionel telling him I would be gone for the night.

I got to Michael's house and a few of our friends were there. We all sat down and talked about the mess I was in. Everyone had an opinion: don't mess with your roommate; leave friends alone; everyone is fair game; if you really love him, you should go after him;

you need to have the talk with him. I was happy when they all left. I just wanted to be alone with Michael. We took off our clothes and cuddled in his bed. We hadn't had sex since the incident and I was starting to think we'd never have sex again. He didn't bring it up and whenever I tried to get a conversation going about it, he always said I wasn't ready. He was right. I didn't really want to have sex with him; I wanted to have sex with Lionel. It had always been Lionel, and it wasn't fair to Michael to pretend like he was Lionel. Michael said I didn't use him because he enjoyed being with me, but we both knew that I used him. Until I could get my head straight about Lionel, I wasn't going to mess with any guys. Michael had given me all the comfort and companionship I could ever ask for from a friend. We fell asleep with me snuggled in his arms.

I opened my eyes in the middle of the night and I wasn't sure what woke me up. I felt a finger poke my arm. "Wake up and get your damn phone!"

I was only somewhat aware of a ringing sound, "Huh? It'll stop in a minute." I sluggishly rolled over trying to go back to sleep, but I felt the same poking sensation on my arm. "What?" I growled at Michael.

"It must be important. It's been ringing for at least ten minutes. Whoever it is keeps hanging up and calling back."

"Okay, okay. I'll get it." My eyes were only partly open when I rolled out of bed and tried to find my phone in the dark. There appeared to be a little bit of light coming from my pants pocket so I bent down and picked up the phone. I looked at my caller id, but there was no name. I picked up the phone and my voice cracked as I said, "Hello."

"You're with him, aren't you?" The voice sounded familiar, but it was somehow different. The voice was hostile, sad, and drunk all at the same time. My eyes shot open and I was fully alert. "Of course you would be. What the hell am I thinking? I'm in bad shape. I need you, and you know we need to talk, but I don't want to talk, I'm scared to talk about it. Something's wrong with me. Will you come get me?" The words were slurred but I thought I understood most of them correctly.

"Where are you?"

"I'm in our room. Where are you? No don't tell me."

An intense feeling of needing to be there for him took over. I jumped in my clothes. I gave Michael the concise version, omitting the fact that something was definitely wrong because Lionel didn't usually drink enough to get drunk. Michael offered to drive me, but I decided to go by myself. I had to face him alone.

Chapter 4

Say it Ain't True

I took a deep breath before I opened the door. I expected to see Lionel knocked out on his bed. He sounded pretty bad when I talked to him. He asked me to come get him like he was out in the street somewhere then he told me he was in our room. I opened the door and was shocked to find Lionel sitting on my bed staring at me.

"You came?" I saw the look of surprise in his eyes. I also saw the red. His eyes were bloodshot and scary looking.

"Of course I came. You needed me." I smiled at him then I closed the door and locked it. I promised myself neither of us would leave the room until we talked. I knew I had driven him to drink. He couldn't deal with having a gay roommate. It was my fault. He ripped his gaze away from me and stared at the floor.

"Man this is fucked up!" He looked back at me and I wasn't sure what I saw in his eyes. The only thing I knew was that he needed me. I should have been comforting him and making it easier for him to say whatever he needed to say to me. I walked over to him and sat next to him. I put my arm around him and pulled him to me. His eyes were focused on the door. I wondered what I should say, but I was scared to say anything to him. We sat in silence for a few minutes. I had a million thoughts racing through my mind. I wondered what I should say to him. And if I should I even bother trying to have a conversation with him while he was drunk? I wondered why he had called me. I finally decided to just say something.

"I'm sorry." He turned to look at me.

"What?"

"I'm sorry for putting you through this. I wish you could have found out another way, but nothing will change who I am. You said you were okay with it, but we don't even talk about it. You act like it never happened."

"Don't you get it!" he screamed. He pulled away from me and jumped up. "It's not you. It's me. It's fucking me! Something's wrong with me! I walked in and saw you with that fucking guy and it felt like you ripped my heart out. I couldn't breathe. I didn't know what was wrong with me!" He turned around and looked at me again. I knew I must have been a sight because I was sure I was white as snow. His words seemed to offer everything I ever wanted to hear. "I'm not gay! I'm not fucking gay! I'm not! I just." He paused for a minute and I could see his mind searching for words. "I just. I don't know. I had this idea that I would come here and we'd fuck around, but instead I find you with him. I'm not gay! I just thought it would be you and me. I thought we could you know." I gave him a questioning look because he was confusing the hell out of me. "I thought we could experiment." He sat down on the bed. "I noticed you checking me out a long time ago. I used to get turned on thinking that you were watching me. I wondered what it would be like to be with you and to hold you and to kiss you. I don't like guys. I just like, I mean liked, you."

I couldn't think of anything brilliant or witty to say. "Wow."

He laughed. "Ain't this some shit! I tell you what's on my fucking heart and that's all you can say? Say something else." We looked in to each other's eyes. "Please."

"I don't know what to say."

"Say you felt something for me, too. Say you were calling that punk Lionel because you wished he was me. Say I'm not crazy to think that there's something between us; that there's always been something between us."

"I'm in love with you." I didn't know why or how the words came out, but they did. The truth came running from my lips like it was on fire. We both sat there in separate states of shock. I was mentally bashing myself for letting such words come out. After a few moments of silence, I realized I was still staring in to his eyes. I wondered if he was having the same conversation in his head that I was having in mine. He started leaning forward. His lips attacked mine and I happily gave in. He pulled back.

He whispered, "You taste good."

"So do you." That was only half true. Most of him tasted like beer, but there was another distinct taste, a taste that was pure him: his taste. His taste was good and intoxicating all by itself.

He pushed me back on the bed and put his lips against mine. His tongue forced its way in my mouth and there was a hint of violence and brutality in his raw passion. There was a small voice in my head that yelled at me to stop, but I had wanted him too long to pass on any affection from him. His tongue returned to his mouth. He bit my bottom lip as he lifted his lips away from mine. It wasn't enough to draw blood, but it did remind me that I was alive and he was real. I wondered if it was an accident, but I knew it wasn't when I felt his teeth scrape my neck. I gasped from the feeling. He replaced his teeth with his tongue and used his tongue to trace along the places he had touched with his teeth. Next he put his soft lips down on my neck and began a suction that was sure to leave a mark. I felt like I was floating above my body looking down at us. I was afraid to move. He slid his tongue up my neck and found my ear. His tongue covered my ear in saliva as it pushed in and out and his hot breath made the wetness tingle as it vibrated between my skin and his lips. No one had ever licked my ear before. It felt weird at first but then it felt okay and kind of nice. "I want you," he whispered. That was when I felt his monster pressing against me. I was scared of what he wanted to do, but I would have done anything to please him. "Let's get naked." He rolled off of me and started taking off his clothes.

"Maybe we should slow down." He gave me a look like I just stabbed him in the back. "I don't want to do this after you've had so much to drink."

"I'm fine. I'm not drunk anymore." He placed a gentle kiss on my lips and said, "I know exactly what I'm doing." Who was I to stop him? I sat up and started taking off my clothes. I kicked off my shoes and pulled off my pants. I was about to pull down my boxers when Lionel stopped me. "Let me help you with that." I was about to offer to help him with his boxers but I looked down and saw his exposed penis. He grinned and placed his hand on my hard-on through my boxers. He started rubbing it and the friction from the fabric of my boxers had me moaning out loud. I closed my eyes and relaxed under his gentle touch. He suddenly pulled away and I opened my eyes in enough time to see his naked butt walk over to his computer. I was about to ask him what the hell he was doing, but I saw him turn on his speakers and I had a good idea what was going on. Within seconds there was a playlist on the screen and music blaring out of his speakers. He walked back to the bed and hopped on it. He leaned close to my ear and I waited for his tongue to make contact, but instead I heard him say, "Now you can scream as loud as you want to." I looked in his eyes and all I saw was lust. I knew then that we were going to have sex that night. I didn't think he could stop himself.

He gave my lips a slight kiss then began making a path down my body. He started pulling down my boxers and I raised my hips to make it easy for him. He pulled them off and threw them across the room. I was losing pre-cum like a leaky faucet. His tongue licked some of my pre-cum and I watched as he swallowed. He licked his lips and leaned up to kiss me. The kiss was a full-fledged attack. It felt like he was trying to fuck my mouth with his tongue. His ferocity was too much for me. I felt overwhelmed by his passion. He took his tongue out of my mouth and said, "Relax." He went down to one of my nipples and sucked on it so hard that I thought he might suck it off then he bit it and I jumped. I never thought I would enjoy someone causing me pain with their teeth, but somehow his love nick made me want him even more.

I felt his hand slide down my body and then I felt a finger going up and down my crack. I spread my legs wide to give him better access. I wanted him to put it in. The finger traced around my hole a few times before finally trying to gain entrance. He slowly stuck the finger inside me. I responded by saying, "Uh."

"Yeah, you like that don't you?"

I looked down and saw the top of his head. He was still at work on my nipples, causing me to wonder if he had really said anything. I moaned a little louder when another finger entered me. His fingers were definitely longer than Michael's, I could feel the difference. His pumping pace with his fingers seemed coordinated with his sucking action on my nipple. "I'm about to cum." I wanted to warn him. His response was to stick in a third finger and increase the speed. I came all over myself and he licked me clean with his tongue. Then I heard the words that I had been both dreading and eagerly awaiting.

"Now it's my turn." He got up and walked over to his drawer. I assumed he was getting lube and a condom, so I took the time to get on all fours. I didn't want to have the option of watching that monster stretching me open. He walked back to the bed and slapped my ass. "Turn over. I want to see your face while I fuck you." He didn't have to tell me twice. I was willing to do whatever he wanted. I turned over, spread my legs and tried to get them as high as I could. My legs immediately came down when I noticed that he didn't have a condom.

"Where's the condom?"

"We don't need one."

"Yes we do, we've both been with other people." What I really meant was, 'You've claimed to have fucked some nasty bitches and I'm not trying to catch anything.'

"Damn that shit! We don't need no fucking condoms! I want to feel everything!" Before I could protest, he was climbing on top of me. He pushed my legs up and let them rest on his shoulders as he lined up his well lubed 10 and a half inch dick. He placed the head at my hole and started to press in. There was a little pop and his head was inside me. "Oh fuck yeah! Oh!" was his response. He began to push in at a pace that was a little faster than I would have liked, but I didn't protest. He didn't go in all the way, but he seemed satisfied. The sensations I felt from having something so big inside me were intense and surprisingly pleasing. He touched the right spot with every thrust and soon we were both moaning and panting and dripping sweat. I didn't want it to stop because I didn't want to remember what it felt like to not have his dick inside me anymore. I wished our lovemaking could last forever, but it didn't. To my surprise, Lionel's dick began to grow inside me and I knew he was about to cum. He came in spurts that blasted my insides. I wondered why I didn't insist on a condom. He collapsed on top of me and whispered, "I love you." He rolled off of me and stood. He walked over to his computer and closed the playlist. He turned off the speakers. "Damn that shit was loud!" I watched as he grabbed his towel, shower shoes and shower basket. He wrapped the towel around his waist, took a quick look in the mirror and headed to the bathroom.

I was in bed wondering what just happened. I was expecting to cuddle with Lionel for a while. After a few minutes, I started to regret the entire night. We shouldn't have done it. It was a mistake. A dumb mistake. I knew it was wrong when we were doing it, but I still went along and every bone in my body was telling me that it was definitely the wrong thing to do. He walked in twenty minutes later and climbed in his bed without a word. I was fairly certain he was also regretting what we had done. I wished I could say something to him, but I couldn't find the words. I should have gotten up and showered, but the weight of our situation had me pinned to my bed. Lionel turned off the light near his bed and said, "Thanks for the action Lucas, I really needed that. You're a good friend."

I almost threw up when I heard Lionel say that. What was he talking about? He made it sound like I had sex with him as his friend and not as the guy he loved. Like I did him a favor by letting him fuck me. I didn't like his tone, but I was too submerged in thought to address it. I fell asleep thinking about us.

I woke up the next morning to find Lionel dressing to go somewhere. "Where are you going?"

"I don't think that's any of your business."

"I think it is after last night." He turned and gave me a look that sent a chill running up and down my spine. "Do we need to talk?"

"There's nothing to talk about. Nothing happened! I was lonely. I needed to fuck something, so I said some things to you that I knew would make you open your legs. You came, I came and that's all it was, end of discussion."

"But."

"Don't say another word about it. It's over!" I had never heard Lionel be so cruel and callous before.

"But." He ran over to me and put his hand around my neck.

"Don't say shit about it. I'm not playing with you, Lucas. I don't want to talk about it!"

I knew he meant business, so I dropped the subject. We sat there in an awkward silence as I replayed all of his words from the night before and tried to reconcile them with his change of heart. There was a knock at the door. Lionel opened it and there was a skinny black girl standing there. She asked him if he was ready and he said almost. He invited her in for a minute and introduced her to me. "Lucas, this is my girlfriend."

Chapter 5

Ouch

Lionel was an asshole! I couldn't ignore it, I couldn't sugar coat it, I couldn't pretend like it wasn't true. He was and I knew it. The past two weeks had been strained and stressful to say the least. Our conversations were empty and all traces of our friendship were gone. We were only remnants of our former selves and it was his fault. He ruined us! He ruined me! God I hated him! No, I didn't mean that. I loved him. Why couldn't I stop thinking about him? He hurt me but I still wanted him.

Everything had changed between us. We didn't work out together anymore. Practice had finally started so I was getting to know some of the guys from the team, but talking to them didn't replace the feelings I have for him. I thought I saw him looking at me a few times in the locker room, but I knew it was probably my imagination.

I was standing in line at practice, waiting for my turn to do the three-man weave. It was finally my turn to go and I grabbed the ball and made the first pass. I was running to get behind the guy I had just passed the ball to, when something hit me on the side of my face. I hit the ground. My eye was stinging so I put my hand on it. My head started throbbing as I tried to stand. I felt dizzy so I sat down on the court. By the time my ass made contact with the floor, I was surrounded by teammates. I felt a hand on my shoulder and I instantly thought of Lionel. I smiled a little thinking that he had come over to check on me, but then the hand rubbed across my back and the person walked around to the front. I saw the shoes and the pants and I knew who it was.

"Are you okay, Son?" Coach Higgins sounded concerned so I knew I must have looked bad.

"I think so, but my eye hurts." I felt liquid running down my face. "Stop pouring water on me. I don't need it."

Coach leaned down in front of me and my good eye looked at him. "Don't panic, but that's not water."

Talk about an idiot move. Never tell someone not to panic and then let them know that they're bleeding profusely. I moved my hand and held it in front of my other eye. The hand was covered in blood. I didn't want to look like a bitch in front of the team, so I fought the urge to scream like a girl. "Shit!" was all I said.

"Somebody go call for help!" Then I heard Coach ask, "Who threw that fucking ball?" I heard someone say it was Lionel and I wanted to cry. "Why would you do that?"

I heard Lionel say, "I was just playing around. I didn't mean to hurt him."

"You threw a ball at his face! What the hell is your problem? You didn't mean to hurt him? Look at him! Look at what you did! Get out of my sight!" I thought he wasn't being harsh enough, but I understood that he probably didn't want to go off too badly on our soon to be star player.

"I want to make sure he's okay. I really didn't mean to hurt him." He sounded like he was crying, but I knew that couldn't be the case.

"Well stop crying and grab a towel!" At least he felt sorry for it. I heard him run off to the side of the court and run back. He pushed Coach aside and kneeled in front of me with the towel. I stared at him, mesmerized by our proximity.

"I got it. Relax." He put the towel on my eye and held it there for a minute. He took the towel away and said, "Wow, that's a nasty cut! I'm so sorry. I didn't mean to hurt you. You have to believe me." The look in his eyes, along with the traces of tears on his face told me that he meant it. Of course he didn't want to hurt me.

"I know." He started walking away and I wondered what was wrong with him. Then there was another set of feet in front of me.

"What happened?" I didn't recognize the voice and I didn't feel like talking. He must have realized that I was not going to answer, because I could feel him look away from me. "Did he fall?"

I heard Lionel say, "I hit him in the head with a ball and then he hit the ground."

"Well it looks like he's going to need stitches. We're going to have to take him to the hospital."

"Can I ride with him?" Lionel seemed worried.

"Well, um, where's the trainer?"

That's when Coach stepped in, "He's not here today."

"Do you want to go with him?"

"Lionel can ride with him if he wants to." Another paramedic was there and the two men helped me on to a gurney. As they were wheeling me out of the gym, I heard Coach saying, "Alright you maggots, someone get the janitor to come clean up this blood, and the rest of you give me laps until we can get back to work. Don't worry about Lucas, he'll be fine."

They put me in the ambulance and Lionel climbed in and sat next to me. At one point during the ride, Lionel reached over and grabbed my hand. I should have been thinking about how he was the one who hit me, but I wasn't. I was thinking of how soft his fingers felt and how nice his hand felt. I squeezed his hand and he squeezed back. He had to let go when we got to the hospital. The paramedics rolled me in and I saw a doctor. I had to explain what happened and he tried to figure out if I had a concussion. He asked me a million questions while a nurse cleaned up my cut. After my stitches were in, the doctor looked at my eyes and asked me some more questions. He made me do a couple of other tests, too. I thought he was trying to be funny, but he explained why he was doing it. He said he had to check my strength, sensation, balance, reflexes and memory. I said, "Whatever."

The doctor told me I could go home but I had to promise that I would rest and come back to the hospital if I felt worse. He told me he had talked to Lionel and Lionel promised to take care of me. How was I supposed to rest when I had Lionel taking care of me? The doctor wanted to put me in a wheelchair so I could be wheeled out, but I refused the chair. I wanted to walk out on my own. Lionel was sitting in the waiting room. He had his head down so I had to tap his shoulder to get his attention. "I'm ready to go."

"You checked out already?"

"Yes."

"Okay, let's go then." He stood and put his arm around me like he was saving me from something. I leaned against him for added support as we walked outside. Lionel waved his arm but nothing happened. I wondered what he was doing, but I didn't care to ask. Then a car pulled out of a parking spot, drove around the parking lot and stopped in front of us. Lionel opened the back door for me and told me I could lie across the backseat. When I got in, I saw the face of the driver. Of course, it was her—his girlfriend. She was such a sweet girl, but I hated her so much. I wanted to be the one with Lionel, not her. My jealousy had never allowed me to get to know her, yet there she was, asking me how I felt and taking me home. I told myself she was doing this for Lionel, not me. Lionel closed the door behind me and got in the front seat. I felt sick when he leaned over and kissed her. "Thanks, Babe." She smiled at him and I wished it was me smiling at him. She was so lucky and she didn't even know it. I had a feeling of regret when I remembered that Lionel had hit me with the ball. I didn't know why it was so hard for me to remember that it was him. I closed my eyes and tried to blink away the bad thoughts about Lionel. Lionel was a good guy. He couldn't have meant to hurt me. He was just fooling around.

Lionel practically carried me to our dorm room. Luckily, he left the girl in the car and told her he would call her later. He pulled back my covers and sat me on my bed. I watched as he pulled off my shoes. He lifted my legs for me and then bundled me up in the covers. I was about to thank him for being so kind, when I heard the familiar sound of my phone ringing. I thought I had left my phone in the locker room. Lionel reached in his pocket and took out my phone. Before I could ask how he got it, he answered it. He started telling the person that I couldn't talk because I had an accident at practice. He omitted the fact that he was the person who threw the ball.

"Who is it?" I asked.

He ignored me and kept talking to the person. "He'll be fine. He has a few stitches, but he seems to be doing a lot better and his color is coming back. He looked like death earlier." There was a pause and I guess he was listening. "Look, he doesn't want to talk to anyone right now. I'll tell him to call you back when he feels better so just relax, okay?" I assumed it must not have been okay because Lionel made a face then turned his back to me. I heard him say, "Look I'm not doing this because I'm jealous of you and him." There was another pause. "I'll tell him to call you back!" The person said something else then Lionel told them, "So what if it was me who threw the ball! I wasn't trying to hurt him and I'm not a jerk! You're the fucking jerk! I told you he would call you back, now goodbye!" He slammed my phone shut.

I didn't have to ask who it was because the conversation made that clear. It must have been Michael. Michael did not like Lionel. He told me Lionel sounded like a closet case and that I shouldn't get involved with Lionel because he would probably play games with my heart before he broke it completely. Michael said it was obvious Lionel didn't feel the same way about me that I felt about him. I told Michael I didn't care and he told me one day I would. Anyway, Michael and Lionel had not talked to each other before and their first conversation didn't sound like it went very well. Lionel turned around and walked to me. He handed me the phone. "Michael?" I asked. I already knew the answer.

"Yep. That guy is such a jerk. He acted like I was trying to keep the two of you apart or something. Like I was a jealous boyfriend, but no matter how much I love you, we're not boyfriends." His words were music to my ears. He loved me. I knew it! You couldn't feel the kind of heat I felt for him if it wasn't reciprocated by the other side. I wanted to call him on it and say, 'Oh, so you do love me?' but I was afraid of chasing him away. It was obvious he needed to take baby steps and I was more than okay with waiting. One day he wouldn't view the term "boyfriend" as offensive. One day he would be mine.

"Thanks for telling him I didn't want to talk. I don't have the energy to deal with his questions."

"I figured that."

"How'd you get my phone?"

"Troy from the team, brought our phones to the hospital. I guess he went in our lockers and got them for us. I thanked him for thinking about us. We wouldn't want to leave that shit in there overnight. You know the mice around here have sticky fingers."

I laughed and my head hurt. "Don't make me laugh."

"Sorry," he said as he turned to walk to his bed.

I knew I shouldn't do it, but part of me was dying to hear the answer. "Lionel." He turned around and looked at me. I wondered if he realized this was the most we had said to each other since the morning after. "Why did you hit me with the ball?"

He backed up and sat down on his bed. "You want the truth?" He looked me dead in my eyes and I didn't want the truth, but I knew I needed to hear it. I prepared my ears for the beating I thought they were about to take.

"Of course I want the truth." There was a long pause. "Well?"

"I hate you. I did it because I hate you." That was not the answer I was planning for, but I wasn't surprised by it either. I turned on my side, with my back facing him, so I could look away from him. "Don't you want to know why?"

"No," I croaked while holding back tears and trying to vanquish all fantasies of us being together. He loved me as a friend but he hated the gay part of me.

I heard him moving across the floor. I listened as he walked towards my bed and kicked off his shoes. He pulled back my covers, but I didn't turn around. I felt his body on my bed and then I felt his arm come around me and pull me close. "I hate you because I can't get you out of my head. You just won't go away! I was watching you in practice today and I couldn't take it anymore. I needed to take my eyes off of you, but I couldn't. When you went to run to the other side, I just lost it. I wanted to make you disappear and before I knew it, I was chucking the ball at your head. I wasn't really trying to hurt you. I just wanted you to be gone. I regretted it the second the ball left my hands. I was just so angry. Why can't I have you?" He sounded choked up, but I was too deep in thought to notice it much.

"You can have me," I whispered.

"No I can't. It's not right. I can't do that to my family or to myself."

The words bounced around in my head for a little while and a few minutes later, I asked, "So you would rather deny it forever?"

"I don't know." He said it so softly that I was afraid to press him. Maybe one day he would be ready to answer that question, but I knew he wasn't ready then. We relaxed for a long time with me cradled in Lionel's arms. He fell asleep and I listened to his light snores as his chest went up and down against my back. 'This could work,' I thought. 'He's just a work in progress.'

I woke the next morning to an empty bed.

Chapter 6

Strange Happenings

Two days after being bopped on the head, I was cleared to resume working out moderately with the team, but not practicing. I was unsure how Lionel would act around me because he had been treating me like a baby since the accident.

I woke up the day after he hit me and he was gone. I thought he had abandoned me, but he returned a few minutes later with breakfast in hand and a smile on his face. He tried to feed me, but I wouldn't let him. We spent the next two days talking like we did in high school. We laughed and just had a good time, but we didn't talk about us. I was beginning to realize that we were both trying to avoid having another conversation about it. Michael came over to visit the first day and he and Lionel exchanged a few words before I sent Lionel to get lunch. Michael wanted me to petition for a new roommate, but I refused. I told him how wonderful Lionel was being and how nice he seemed. Michael said Lionel sounded like a classic abuser to him. I told Michael he didn't know Lionel the way I did. Lionel was a harmless guy. Michael left when Lionel returned with the food, but he called to check on me a few times. My mother called and I told her I had an accident at practice, but I didn't have the heart to tell her Lionel hit me on purpose.

When I walked in to the locker room for my first post accident workout, I couldn't stop thinking about Lionel. Lionel was walking next to me with his hand resting gingerly on the small of my back. The other guys looked over and most of them welcomed me. No one seemed to notice how close Lionel and I were standing. Lionel walked me to my locker and opened it for me. He smiled when I thanked him. He opened my gym bag and sat it down on the bench then he watched as I undressed and changed my clothes. I moved too fast and I almost lost my balance, but his arms were around me as soon as I began to fall. He stood me up straight and we looked in to each other's eyes and it was a perfect kiss moment, but no where near a coming out moment. We both gave sheepish smiles and Lionel let me go. He cleared his throat and stepped back. I knew he wanted to kiss me and I knew I wanted to kiss him, but I would never kiss him in front of our teammates, and he was too much of a punk to kiss me anyway. I knew I was blushing, so I turned and faced my locker and prayed that no one noticed. Lionel moved to his locker and changed his clothes.

I looked at myself in the small mirror in my locker. My eye was still swollen, but it didn't hurt much. It definitely looked worse than it felt. I put my bag in the locker along with my regular clothes and I shut the locker.

Some guy from the team walked over to me and put his hand on my shoulder. He said, "Glad to have you back."

"Glad to be back." He walked away from me and left the locker room.

I looked at Lionel as he pulled his shirt over his head. He was so beautiful. He caught me watching him and he looked away. I felt the sexual tension between us and I couldn't deny that it was getting stronger. I knew he loved me. His actions made that clear. He might have been afraid to love me, but he couldn't deny that he did. He had been so sweet, tender, and loving over the past few days. I kept watching him dress because I was no longer afraid of what he would do. I sat there taking in every movement he made as he changed his clothes and put on his shoes. It seemed like it was just me and him and I couldn't take my good eye off of him. I still hadn't figured out why I loved him, but the feeling I got when I was around him let me know for sure that I did.

He tied his shoestring and looked at me. He smiled and asked, "Are you ready?"

"Yeah." He walked over to me and grabbed my hand. 'How gay,' I thought, but I knew he was holding my hand like I was a child and not like I was his lover. He let go of my hand when we reached the door. We took a few steps in the hallway and I felt Lionel's hand on my back again. I had to contain my emotions as we walked in the weight room. Lionel walked me to the leg press.

"You want to start here?"

"Sure." He put the weights on and hovered over me like I might break a bone or something. The rest of the workout was more of the same. We went from machine to machine with him hovering over me and babying me. I should have been annoyed, but I was tickled pink because I loved every second of it. I loved the way he guided me from machine to machine with his hand on my back. I loved the way he watched me and counted my reps out loud. I loved the way he praised me no matter how poorly I did. He did a lot more reps than I did at all the machines, but he treated me like I was the strongest. The workout put me in a great mood.

We showered after practice and changed in to our regular clothes. As we were leaving the gym, Lionel told me he had a surprise for me. He told me he was taking me out to dinner and he put a blindfold on me. "Trust me," he said.

"I do." I tucked my arm inside his and he started walking. I did trust him. I wished I could see the expressions on everyone's faces with us walking like that. I could only imagine the thoughts that must be going through people's minds.

When we reached the outside, I heard someone yell, "Lionel, I didn't know you were in to blind dudes!"

He shouted back, "Only on the weekend."

The guy must have walked over to us because his voice was much closer when he asked, "What's up man? What the hell are you doing? Isn't this your roommate?"

"Yes. I'm taking him to dinner, and he can't know where we're going so I had to blindfold him."

"That's a little gay, don't you think?"

"Well what do you want me to do? I don't want him to see where we're going."

"I was referring to the dinner thing. Two guys having a romantic dinner together?"

"It isn't romantic. We're friends. Friends can eat together."

"I guess, but I gotta tell you that you guys look like two fags." He laughed and to my horror, Lionel laughed with him. "Is this to make up for that shiner you gave him the other day?"

Lionel laughed again. "Yeah, something like that." I was hurt that he was laughing about it and I was also a little offended.

I decided to speak up. "Well, whoever you are, we have to go now."

The mystery guy said okay and told Lionel he would catch him later.

Once we took a few steps, Lionel said, "You didn't have to be so rude."

"Well he didn't have to be so ignorant."

"He was just joking. Come on man, calm down."

"Well he wasn't very funny to me."

"Relax, I want you to have a good time, so put that smile back on your face and let's enjoy the evening."

I kept walking with him. We got on a bus and took a ride to somewhere. My thoughts moved to what was awaiting me and I forgot about the stupid guy from school. I started smiling and fantasizing of where the evening would lead. Lionel grabbed my arm for me to stand. "Are we there already?" I asked.

"Yes."

"Oh, so it's not far from school?"

"Stop trying to figure out where we are and just chill. Now hold on to me."

"Okay."

We walked off the bus and it felt strange to be dependent on him to tell me when to step. He was better the second time though because I almost fell trying to get on the bus, but getting off the bus was easy. We walked for a few minutes and I heard lots of people talking around us.

We walked in somewhere and my nose was filled with the most wonderful smells. I knew it must have been an Italian restaurant. He knew I loved Italian food, especially the pastas. Some one said, "Welcome to" and I couldn't really decipher the name of the restaurant, "would you like smoking or non-smoking?"

"I have reservations."

The perky voice asked, "You do? What name is it under?"

"Lionel."

"Oh okay. I see your name. Must be a special evening. Right this way, Sir." I knew my cheeks were crimson, but the way she said 'must be a special evening' was so suggestive that I had to blush from the x-rated thoughts that invaded my head. We started walking, which proved difficult. I hit a few chairs, but I was never tempted to take off the blindfold. I wanted the surprise to be unspoiled. "I hope everything is to your liking." I heard her as her heels walked away from us. It sounded kind of quiet so I was wondering if everyone was staring at us. I didn't feel like I was being watched, but I started to get a little paranoid. Before I could ask what was going on, Lionel removed my blindfold. I was standing in a room with only one table. The table was set for two, with romantic candles and a bunch of roses on one of the plates.

"Are these for me?" I asked as I walked to the roses and picked them up.

"Yes."

We sat down at the table and I picked up a menu. I put the menu down when I saw the prices. "Lionel, what are we doing here? You know you can't afford this!"

"Don't worry about it. It's covered."

"How?"

"I have my ways. Now order whatever you want." He opened his menu. I opened my mouth to say something, but he knew me oh too well. Without looking at me, he raised a finger and said, "Not another word about the prices."

I left it alone and opened my menu. I was about to tell him I wanted some lasagna when I started hearing this voice. The voice sounded familiar and like the voice of someone I hated, but it couldn't be her. I told myself that until she walked in from some door. She had on black pants, a white shirt, and a name tag. She ran to Lionel and he stood.

"Hey, Babe." He put his arms around her and I felt like I was going to puke. He kissed her and I had to look away. I couldn't believe I had been so dumb. I thought we were on a date. In my mind, I saw us toasting our love over a great meal, but I should have known it was too good to be true. "Thanks for letting us eat here."

"You know you're welcome. My uncle says the meal is free. He'll do anything for his favorite niece." She giggled and showed all of her pearly white, perfectly straight teeth. He leaned down and kissed her on the cheek. She giggled louder then she remembered I was in the room. She turned and looked at me. "I hope you're feeling better."

"Yes," was all I could muster at the moment.

"You know Lionel feels horrible about what he did. He would never try to hurt you. You're his best friend."

"Oh."

"Anyway, I'll be your waitress for this evening so what would you like to eat?" I wanted to tell her I had lost my appetite, but I just sat there looking stupid. I looked down at the roses sitting beside my plate. They were beautiful. I felt the tears building up in my eyes. "Aw, I knew you would like the roses," she said as she walked over to me. "I thought they were a little gay at first, but when Lionel told me that you were gay, I thought they would be perfect." I didn't know if I should thank her or smack her. Since when were roses gay and why would Lionel tell her I was gay? She wrapped her arms around me and I let loose. I put my arms around her and cried. She put one hand on the back of my head and rubbed it gently. How could I hate her when she was so sweet? I cried for a few seconds before I gathered myself and pulled away. I wiped my face with one of the napkins and stood.

Lionel was still standing. I looked at him and said, "I've made a complete fool of myself. I just want to go home." I was about to walk out the door and escape the room when Lionel grabbed me and threw me up against the wall. It wasn't violent, but it was forceful.

"Look, you haven't made a fool of yourself, but you will if you leave like this." He relaxed his grip and his eyes begged me as his mouth said, "Stay." My love for him overpowered my brain. He waited for my answer.

"What the hell is going on?" We both looked over and saw Taniqua staring at us. The look in her eyes told me that her brain was processing something.

Lionel responded, "Nothing's going on."

"Then what was that look about?" Her voice was filled with such venom that her accusation almost sounded like a threat.

"It was nothing, Baby. What is wrong with you? What kind of fucked up question is that?"

"I just."

"You just what?" He sounded like he could hit her.

"I thought I saw something. I'm sorry." Her voice was trembling and I knew I heard the unmistakable vibrations of fear.

"Maybe we should leave." He roughly grabbed my arm and started pushing me towards the door. When we reached the door, he stopped and turned around. "Thank you for setting the table. I wish we could have stayed for dinner, but Lucas is obviously a little too emotional for that. I'll call you later."

"Okay." She sounded submissive and I wondered if that was how I sounded around Lionel.

Lionel held my arm roughly until we were outside. He shoved me away from him and said, "You want to go home? Let's go!"

Chapter 7

Another Side

The ride home on the bus was horrible. I was afraid of what Lionel was going to do to me. Every time the bus stopped I had thoughts of getting off and running away. I knew I should run directly to Michael. He was the only one who would know what to do, but I was scared to move. I didn't realize my knee was shaking until I felt Lionel's hand on it.

"Stop it!" he commanded in a forceful whisper. I closed my eyes for a second so I wouldn't pee on myself. My shaking stopped immediately. Every limb of my body was frozen. I don't remember thinking anything after that. I must have zoned out. I was blankly staring out the window when Lionel pulled me up and pushed me towards the exit. The walk to our dorm was faster than I ever remembered it being. I stood outside our dorm room shaking as Lionel unlocked our door. He flung the door open, grabbed my arm, and basically threw me in the room. He locked the door. He turned and looked at me and I looked at him. He started walking towards me and I took a few steps back. "What the hell is your problem?" he shouted.

"Nothing." My voice cracked and I looked at the floor. I felt like my knees might buckle at any moment. I stepped back until I reached my bed and then I sat down. By the time I looked at him, he had closed the gap between us. He was standing directly in front of me. I watched as he lifted his hand. It seemed like slow motion as his hand approached my face. I flinched. His hand stopped in midair.

"Do you think I'm going to hit you?" the shock in his voice was a little confusing to me. Of course I thought he was going to hit me. What was I supposed to think?

I was able to eke out a weak, "Yes."

His hand came towards me again, but this time he said, "I'm not going to hit you." I felt his hand on my chin. He directed my face up, but I kept my eyes cast downward. "Look at me," he said. I couldn't deny him. I looked in to his eyes and he was a stranger to me. I felt the tears welling up in my eyes. Looking at him was too painful. I moved to look away from him, but he wouldn't let me move my face. I settled for moving my eyes instead. I saw his computer and the image on it caught my attention. He must have touched it when he walked across the room. The screensaver was a picture of us from high school. We were both wearing our uniforms and he had his arm around my shoulders and we both had big smiles on our faces. Before I could remember when the picture was taken, the screen changed and a picture of our high school team popped up. I knew exactly where to find us. We were both in the back, standing next to each other, still smiling. I wished we could go back to those happy times; those memories, those moments when it felt like we could take on the world and win, but those times were gone. I reluctantly let a tear fall down my cheek. Lionel's pinky caught it before it could reach my chin and fall. I looked in to his eyes again and I swear I saw traces of the Lionel I knew. I was mesmerized as he placed his pinky in his mouth. He sucked his pinky for a second while he stared at me. I wasn't sure if he was trying to seduce me or take away my pain.

Once he took his pinky out of his mouth, he spoke again. "Don't cry Lucas. I would never hurt you. You should know that." I wanted to ask him how I would know that, but I was still afraid of him. His words were incapable of bringing me comfort. We both sat there not saying a word. I wanted to tell him to let go of my face, but my vocal chords refused to make a sound. My throat felt dry so I gathered up saliva in my mouth and swallowed. The vibrations from my throat got Lionel's attention and the silence was interrupted by a smacking sound as Lionel kissed my forehead. He started planting angel kisses all over my face and I let him. He paused for a second as his lips hovered over mine. I finally realized that I should pull back but his hand was still holding my face. I closed my eyes as his lips began to get closer. I felt the contact throughout my whole body and that scared me. His tongue pressed against my lips and my lips parted without my permission. He released my chin from his grasp and pushed me back on the bed. My senses returned when my head hit the bed.

I pulled away from the kiss and tried to push him off of me. "Get off!" I yelled.

"We both know this is what you want, so just shut up and enjoy it." My brain didn't register what he said until his lips crashed in to mine again. His tongue tried to force access to my mouth but I kept my lips closed tightly and started shaking my head and trying to push him off. "Stop fighting this," he said before his lips made contact with my neck. He started sucking on my neck and I couldn't believe he wasn't listening to me. I wondered if he was going to force himself on me.

Tears fell from my eyes and I started really struggling. "Get off of me!" To my surprise, he moved. He stood up and looked down at me.

"What is wrong with you? I know you want this! Why are you fighting me?" I opened my mouth to answer him but the loud knocks on the door quickly grabbed my attention. Lionel looked at me for a second, I watched as he adjusted his hardon and walked to the door. I sat up and wiped away my tears. He opened the door and I saw Henry, our resident advisor.

"Is everything okay?" Henry asked.

"Yes." Lionel said with a little irritation in his voice.

"Well, some of the other residents reported shouting"

Lionel cut him off. "That's bullshit and you know it! Shouting? We just got back a few minutes ago. How the hell would anyone have enough time to complain?"

Henry seemed unbothered by Lionel's abruptness. "Fine, I was walking by the door and I heard you two shouting. It sounded like you were fighting."

"No, we weren't. We were just playing around. Sorry if we were too loud. We'll try to be a quieter." Lionel moved to close the door, but Henry was having none of that. Henry pushed Lionel aside and walked over to me.

"Are you okay Lucas?"

"Yes, I'm fine." I hoped that I sounded normal, but I knew I didn't.

"Are you sure? I can tell that you've been crying." He looked at me for a moment, probably trying to gauge my response. He leaned down and whispered in my ear, "We can talk about this in private if you don't want to discuss it in front of Lionel." He stood up tall again and I looked over at Lionel who was still standing by the door.

"Thanks for your concern Henry, but everything is fine. We just had a little disagreement, nothing to worry about. We'll keep it down." He looked at me like I was lying through my teeth.

Henry put his hand on my shoulder and said, "If you need to talk about anything, and I mean anything, just come knock on my door." He sounded like he was hitting on me, but I wasn't sure until he winked at me and whispered, "You could do so much better than him." When he said that I knew he must have heard a lot of our conversation.

"How long were you listening?" I whispered back.

"Long enough to know that you're too good for him and he was trying to force you to do something you didn't want to do."

"Oh, well everything is okay." I said a little louder, making sure Lionel could hear me. "I'll talk to you later Henry and thank you for checking on us."

"Okay." Henry walked to the door.

I watched as Henry whispered something to Lionel and walked out. Lionel yelled behind him, "Mind your own damn business!" and slammed the door. He locked it and walked over to his computer to turn on the music. He turned his attention to me and under the cover of music he asked, "What did you say to him?"

"You heard what I said."

"I didn't hear everything, the two of you were whispering about something, now tell me what it was."

"Nothing. It was nothing." I glanced at his eyes and quickly looked away.

"Don't lie to me! I know you said something to him. Do you know what he said to me as he was leaving?" I shook my head. "He said, 'You need to learn how to treat him before someone takes him away from you.' What was that about? Did you tell him that I fucking wanted you or something?"

"No, I didn't say anything to him. He heard us."

"You mean he was fucking eavesdropping! That little bastard! I ought to go kick his ass for hitting on you right in front of me."

"Calm down Lionel!" As I said that, something snapped in me. "Where the hell do you get off being jealous because some guy is showing me interest? You don't care about me and Michael, so why"

He cut me off. "Why would I care about you and Michael when all you do with him is pretend that he's me?"

I didn't follow his logic. My mouth kept moving. "Don't cut me off, Lionel! Let me finish." His lips parted to say something, but I stopped him. "Please."

"Fine, talk." He folded his arms and sat on his computer desk.

"Why do you care about Henry hitting on me? You don't give a shit about me anyway, so what's the problem? All you do is use me. Look at tonight. You acted like you were taking me some place wonderful and instead you took me to the restaurant where your fucking girlfriend works! Talk about mixed signals. This morning you were my hero and tonight you're the sole source of my pain. How fucked up is that? But you know what, I don't blame you. It's my fault for giving you that power. I should have given up on us after you used me just so you could get off. I don't know why I can't seem to let go." I reached up to wipe my face and felt tears streaming down. "I'm just wasting my tears. You're not worth it! You're not worth any of it! You don't want me, that's for sure, so why can't someone else have me? You have no right to be jealous of Henry." I wiped away my last few tears and looked at Lionel. He was crying too.

"I love you."

"No you don't, if you loved me, you wouldn't toy with me."

"Don't tell me how I feel! I do love you. I always have! When we did it, I wasn't using you to get off. I wanted you, but it was too much for me, I'm not gay! I mean I'm not supposed to be gay. I couldn't handle what I felt so I tried to hurt you and push you away. I do love you and I don't know why. I have tried so hard to stop, but

I can't. I just can't. At the same time, I'm not ready to be with you. Why can't you wait for me?" I started laughing. "What's so funny?"

"You want me to wait for you while you stick your dick wherever you please and I sit here like I'm celibate or something?" I took a breath and I started shaking my head. "God, you are so full of shit!" I stood, grabbed a bag and started throwing some clothes in it.

"What are you doing?" I noticed his tears were gone.

"I'm going to spend the night at Michael's."

He walked over to me and grabbed my arm. "Don't leave."

"Give me one good reason why I shouldn't."

"I'll dump Taniqua."

Chapter 8

Goodbye Taniqua?

I grabbed his phone and handed it to him. "Do it then!"

"Now?" he asked.

"Yes."

"But I don't know what to tell her. Why don't I wait until the morning?"

I don't know why his hesitancy angered me. "Fine, do whatever the hell you want to do! I know you, Lionel! Tonight you say wait until the morning, tomorrow it'll be wait until the next day, and the next thing I know, months will have passed and we'll still be in the same fucking spot!" I grabbed my half-packed bag. "Well, no thank you."

"I won't let you leave." He grabbed my arm again and this time he tightened his grip.

"You can't stop me," I said as I ripped my arm away.

"I'll do it! Okay? I'll call her right now and tell her it's over, but please don't leave." I couldn't help but feel a little sympathy for him, especially when he dropped to his knees. "Please don't leave me. I'm begging you. Please don't." His tears started to fall again and that was all it took to weaken me.

"Don't cry, Lionel. It's okay. I won't leave you." I rubbed my fingers across his head.

He looked up at me. "I'll do it! I'll call her right now." His voice trembled.

"You don't have to call her right now. Take a few minutes to get yourself together and I'll help you figure out what to tell her."

It took Lionel about five minutes to calm down enough for us to make a plan. He turned up his cell so I could hear what Taniqua was saying. I sat down next to him and he called her.

"Hello," she said. I was surprised at how well I heard her.

"Hey, Niqua."

"Oh, hey Baby. What are you doing?"

"Um, I need to talk to you about something."

"Is it about Lucas? Is he okay?" the concern in her voice made me want to cry for her.

"No, it's not about Lucas. It's about us."

"Us? What about us?" She sounded worried.

"I think we need to break up, because this isn't working for me." He was cold and callous when he said it.

"What? You can't be serious!" I could tell she was starting to cry.

"I am. It's over." Wow, he was cruel. The plan was for him to let her down gently, but he was definitely not on that page.

"What did I do? Why are you doing this to me?" She sounded so pitiful.

"Look, you knew when this first started that it wouldn't last. I'm too much man for just one person. Come on now Baby, you know that. Now, it's been fun and you've been great, but it's time to move on." I didn't know whether to laugh or smack him, because his voice changed to some sort of smooth talking player type voice and it was funny, but at the same time, what he was saying was mean and he needed to be slapped for that because it was wrong.

"Oh my God! Oh my God! I know what it is!" I wondered what was going through her head, but I didn't have to wait too long. "It's Lucas, isn't it? I saw the way you two looked at each other tonight! I knew it! You're a fucking faggot! Both of you!"

I watched the expression change on Lionel's face. "What the fuck! Bitch I ain't nobody's fucking fag! I was trying to let your ass down easy, but if want to go there, we can fucking go there. I don't want you! I'm sick of fucking you. I'm ready to move on. Now get off my fucking dick, bitch!" He hung up the phone.

She called him right back, but he ignored it. When she called two more times, he turned off his phone. I didn't know what to say to him.

Lionel and I got in to an argument about how he handled Taniqua and we decided to just go to sleep and sort things out in the morning. I woke up at about 3:00am because of knocking on the door.

"Open the fucking door Lionel!" Then the knocking turned to banging and I assumed she was kicking the door. "Open the fucking door!" I was wondering who the hell let her in to the dorm and for the first time ever, I wished that our dorm had a curfew. I sat up on my bed and looked over at Lionel. Lionel was standing in the middle of the room in his boxers. He looked over at me.

"Should I go out there," he whispered.

"How long has she been here?" I asked.

"I'm not sure, but I've been woke for about the last two minutes of it. Where's Henry when you need him?"

I laughed a little. "I don't know man. I don't know."

"Well?"

"Well, what?"

"Should I go out there?"

Before I could answer, I heard Taniqua say, "I can hear you in there motherfucker! Now open the goddamn door!"

I was about to tell Lionel not to open the door, but he started walking towards it. "This bitch is crazy!" he said as he reached for the doorknob. I was scared of what was waiting for him on the other side of that door, but he didn't seem to care much.

He opened the door and closed it behind him. I heard some whispering then Lionel came back in the room. I watched him grab some clothes. "What are you doing?" I asked.

"I have to go talk to her."

"By yourself? Is that safe?"

"She won't hurt me. I'll be fine, now go back to sleep." I watched in silence as he put on his clothes and walked out the door. I knew I wouldn't get any sleep that night, so I got up and did some homework.

Lionel came home around 9 am. He said everything was handled and their relationship was over. A little voice in my head told me he was hiding something, but I wanted to believe him so I didn't question it.

ALionel and I spent the next three weeks trying to sort out our feelings, which was another way of saying that I was waiting for Lionel to come around and realize how much he cared for me. Lionel had been super sweet and a great person to be around. He made me feel good about myself. He was always complimenting me and he gave me massages sometimes when we got back from practice.

He bought me flowers a few times, and we went on our first real date.

He took me out to dinner at this nice restaurant with no waitresses named Taniqua. During the date, Lionel told me, "I'm not gay, I just like you. You're the only guy I've ever had the hots for." I tried to get him to talk about it some more, but he refused to say anything else on that issue. The rest of the date consisted of light conversation. Overall, it was a beautiful evening that ended with a tender kiss on the lips.

We went on a few other dates, but nothing compared to the first one. The gentle kiss that he planted on my lips that night played again and again in my head. It would have been the perfect first kiss, if it was our first kiss. The rest of our dates were equally as nice, but nowhere near the same emotional connection. I kept wondering when he would make it official between us. He never went on more than one date with a girl unless he made her his girlfriend. I was hoping to be treated the same, but I wasn't as fortunate. Lionel violated his first date rule with me. Lionel was the kind of guy who didn't call a girl back if she didn't put out on the first date, but he expected nothing from me. I tried to take it further than just a kiss, but he refused. I didn't know why his refusal bothered me, but it did. It rubbed me the wrong way. Speaking of things that rubbed me the wrong way, Lionel still talked to Taniqua. It really bothered me and I told him that, but he didn't seem to care so what could I do about it? The two seemed to have a good friendship going and I didn't want to be the insecure, jealous type. I wanted Lionel to be happy and having her as a friend made him happy. She was our biggest issue, but we didn't talk about her much.

So, I was sitting in my room trying to study when I heard a knock at the door. I opened it and there was Taniqua. "Lionel's not here." I said it in the nicest voice I could force out.

"I'm not here for him. I need to talk to you." She walked in my room before I could invite her in.

I closed the door. "So what do you want to talk to me about?"

"You need to leave Lionel alone."

"Huh? What are you talking about? Lionel and I are just friends."

"We both know that's not the truth. He denies it, but I know he tried to dump me because of you."

"What do you mean tried to dump you? Are you two still together?"

"Yes. That's why I'm here. You need to leave my man alone so we can be a happy family. His child needs him."

"Child? What child?" I asked bewildered and in shock.

"Oh, he still hasn't told you that I'm pregnant?" She forced an innocent look on her face, but her eyes told me that she was doing all of it on purpose. She was trying to hurt me. "I thought he would have told you by now. He's known for three weeks."

"Well he hasn't mentioned anything so I guess it's just not that important to him." I didn't know why I started being bitchy towards her. It wasn't me and she wasn't the one I was upset with. I didn't want to fight her for Lionel.

"Oh, it's important to him! He went to the doctor with me the other day and he keeps telling me how much he loves me and that we're always going to be together and how he wouldn't leave his child and"

"Why are you telling me this?"

"Because I knew he wouldn't. Look, I know you want him, and I know that part of him wants you, so I'm coming to you now, woman to, well you know, I'm coming to you to tell you to back off and let him be with his family."

"What? Do you seriously think I believe a word you're saying? Lionel would never tell you that you'd always be together. I know him better than that, and I'm not going to stop being friends with him, just because you're afraid that he might want me. I can't do anything about your insecurities. Now if that's all, you can leave." I flashed a small smile. I pointed to the door and said, "You know the way out."

She started walking towards the door. When she got to the door, she opened it and then she stopped. She turned around and told me, "I'd leave him alone if I were you. Don't say I didn't warn you." Then she left.

I closed the door behind her and locked it and got in my bed to cry. How could Lionel do that to me? And was she trying to threaten me, or was she really trying to warn me about Lionel? A few minutes later, I heard the door unlock and Lionel walked in. I turned to look at him, and he dropped his bag when he saw my face. He closed the door and said, "What's wrong?"

"Taniqua stopped by." He suddenly looked sick.

Chapter 9

Two Steps Forward

I was sitting in Michael's living room sipping on hot cocoa as Michael tried to soothe me by lightly rubbing his hand up and down my back.

"Calm down Lucas and tell me what happened." He put his arm around me. "Come on, just tell me. It's okay." His voice was so sweet and tender and for a moment I wished that I loved him instead of Lionel. Things would have been so easy with Michael. He knew how to take care of me, and I knew he would never intentionally hurt me. He wasn't like Lionel.

I felt my eyes begin to water. "I can't tell you. It's horrible! It's just horrible. I don't want to tell you."

"You need to tell me." I sat in silence, so he continued. "I'm not trying to push you, but I need to know what happened so I can help you. You can stay here as long as you want, and I won't judge you, no matter what you tell me. Now, tell me what happened or I'll ask Lionel." Hearing Lionel's name made me look over at Michael. I watched his other hand as it reached across his body before he placed his fingers under my chin. "Please tell me."

"I can't."

He slowly grabbed the cup out of my hand and put it on the table. "Yes, you can." He leaned back on the sofa and pulled me back with him. I rested my head on his chest and listened to his heartbeat and allowed the rhythm to calm me even more. I wanted to tell him everything and before I knew it my mouth opened and the run-in with Taniqua came out. "Wow. What did Lionel say when you asked him about it?"

"Well, let me tell you the rest of the story." I began telling him everything that happened.

"A few minutes after Niqua left, I was in my bed crying. I heard the door open and Lionel walked in. He knew something was wrong right away.

Lionel asked me, "What's wrong?"

I said, "Taniqua stopped by." He suddenly looked sick.

"What did she say?"

"She told me."

"She told you?"

"Yes, she told me everything." I sat up in bed.

"Everything?"

My frustration got the best of me. "Is there a fucking echo in here?"

He opened his mouth to say something but he closed it before any words came out. We stared at each other in silence. "I'm sorry," he finally said. "I should have told you."

"Why did you lead me on? You knew you didn't want me! How could you do this to me again?" I wished the tears would stop, but they kept falling.

"Is that what you think?" He rushed over to my bed and tried to put his arm around me. I pushed him away. "I'm not leading you on, I do want you. You should know that."

"So you want both of us?"

"No! I don't want Niqua. I want you and she knows that. That's why she came over here and told you that shit. She knew I was waiting to tell you because I was scared." He gave a small chuckle. "That bitch has been playing me this whole time. I thought we were friends, but she was fucking playing me."

I felt a little relief to hear that they weren't together, but then I thought about their poor baby being born to a single mother. "What about the baby?"

"What baby?"

"Taniqua told me she was pregnant."

"That's what she told you? That bitch ain't pregnant! She told me she was three weeks ago, but she's not."

I relaxed some when I heard him say that. I couldn't believe Taniqua had told such lies, but for some reason, I wasn't surprised. I let him put his arms around me, and I relaxed in his embrace before my mind trapped some of the words that were replaying in my head. I pulled away from him. "What were you waiting to tell me then?"

"Huh?"

"You said you were waiting to tell me something because you were scared. I need to know what it is."

"I don't know how to tell you. Wait a second." He stood up and walked over to his dresser. He dug in the top drawer and took out a prescription bottle. He walked over to me and handed me an empty bottle. I saw his name on it. I saw 'to be taken twice daily.' I saw a doctor's name, and I saw the drug's name.

"Doxycycline? What's this for?" I asked.

"Chlamydia."

"What?"

"I have, no, I had Chlamydia. Taniqua gave it to me. We went to the doctor three weeks ago because she told me she was pregnant, and she wasn't, but she did have Chlamydia. She was going to the doctor to get some tests and make sure she was clean." He gave a nervous laugh. "That manipulative bitch knew she wasn't pregnant."

I couldn't say anything to him. I wanted to, but I couldn't. My mind was running in fifty different directions. 'If he had Chlamydia, did that mean I had it too? We didn't use protection. Could that kill me? Why wouldn't he tell me when he first found out? I wouldn't have been mad. I would have gone to get tested. Why did he hide it from me? Could I get it from anal sex?' My last thought sailed away from my lips. "Can you get it from anal sex?"

"Yes, and you might have it. I had it and I didn't know until I got tested. They call it a silent disease or some shit like that because a lot of people don't have symptoms. I'm sorry, but I didn't know how to tell you."

"Am I going to die?"

He laughed, "No, you just need to get tested and if you have it you'll get a prescription and it will go away. So don't worry, you won't die."

"Good because I'm going to kill you!" I hissed as I lunged at him. I started swinging my fists wildly and was surprised to find that he was pretty good at dodging blows. "Stop moving!" I yelled at him. I saw this look in his eyes that I had never seen before and he stopped moving just in time for me to connect with his jaw. I hadn't hit him that hard, but it did turn his head a little. He looked at me as he rubbed his cheek. I think we were both in shock. His eyes told me that I shouldn't have done that. They screamed at me that I had hurt him in a way I would never understand, but I was pleased with what I saw. I wanted to hurt him. He didn't love me, he couldn't love me.

"I'm sorry," he said before he ripped his eyes away from mine. He was too late though because I had already seen his tears forming. He kicked off his shoes, got in his bed and faced the wall. I watched him shake a little as he cried. I wanted to hold him and tell him it was okay, but it wasn't. He lied to me. He schemed behind my back. He didn't tell me he had an STD. How could he do that to me?

I grabbed my bag and started packing it because I knew I couldn't live with him anymore. As I was packing, I thought about all the moments over the last three weeks that had led up to that point. I no longer wondered why he didn't want to have sex with me. I threw enough clothes in my bag to last a week and I looked over at Lionel. Lionel had turned around and he was staring at me. I felt guilty for leaving him like that because he looked like he might need me. I caught a glimpse of something hiding behind his eyes and it tugged at my heart strings, but I still grabbed my bag of clothes and a couple of my books and walked out the door. I was surprised when he didn't say anything as I left. And that's it. That's what happened."

My eyes were dry by the time I finished telling Michael what happened. He pulled me closer to him and I knew I was a blubbering mess, but I accepted his invite. He placed a gentle kiss on the top of my head.

"Is that everything Sweetie?" he asked as his hand started rubbing my arm.

"Yes."

"Well that's not so bad then, now is it? I was expecting a grand story of how you caught him cheating on you with Taniqua, but now I find out that you're cheating yourself."

"What?"

"You heard me, you're cheating yourself. You move out because he doesn't tell you he has an STD, but you stay when he assaults you with a basketball? At least I can sort of understand the STD thing. It's definitely hard to tell someone you care about that you may have infected them with anything other than love. You're not innocent in this either, you should have used a condom. You could have HIV right now instead of Chlamydia. You should both be counting your blessings."

"That's not exactly what I wanted to hear."

"I know, but we're closer than lies so I'm telling you the truth. It's not like I told you that dress didn't make you look fat."

"What the hell are you talking about? I've never worn a dress before in my life."

"It's an expression. I mean I'm not going to tell you something just because it makes you feel better, because that's not fair to you, and as far as the dress thing, well, there's a first time for everything." I turned in just enough time to catch the smirk on his face. He really was cute, but my eyes were for Lionel, and Lionel alone. "Call him."

"Why?"

"You need to talk to him."

"But I don't want to talk to him. I just want to go to sleep. Now shut up and let me rest."

Michael pulled away from me. "You need to call him and talk to him. I'm not a big Lionel fan, and we both know that, but this seems like something the two of you can work out. You said he's been wonderful lately, well, until this point, and the look you get in your eyes when I say his name tells me that you still love him, so call him."

"What would I say to him?"

"Start with sorry for hitting you and then go from there."

"May I still stay here tonight?"

"Of course you can. Now I'm going to my bedroom to give you some privacy. Try to be a little understanding, but don't be too gentle, because he did lie to you." He walked towards his room and a few seconds later, I heard his door close.

I pulled out my cell and called my dorm room. There was no answer. I called Lionel's cell and there was no answer there either. I felt a sense of relief that I had a small reprieve from talking to him. I sat on the sofa trying to think about what Michael told me. Was I wrong to be so upset? I didn't feel like I was, but if Michael thought I was overreacting, he was probably right. My thoughts were interrupted by a knock at the door.

"Michael, someone's here." I yelled as I got up and walked towards Michael's bedroom door. He opened the door and looked at me.

"Did you talk to Lionel?"

"No, he wouldn't answer."

"Alright, I'll send whoever it is away so we can talk, okay?"

"Okay."

I went and sat down on the sofa as Michael opened the door. "What are you doing here?" he asked the person on the other side. I could make out the sound of whispering. I heard Michael say, "Well, I guess you can come in for a few minutes." Then he whispered something else.

I sat on the sofa staring blankly at the television and wondering what Michael and his company were going to do. Michael stepped back inside the room and the person at the door walked in. It was Lionel, carrying a bouquet of roses. I looked in his eyes and there was that look again.

Chapter 10

Expect the Unexpected

Michael left the room to give us some privacy. Lionel stood in front of me shifting his weight from side to side every few seconds.

Finally, he held out the roses. "I'm sorry." I knew his apology was genuine, but it seemed like every time I turned around he was sorry for something.

"I don't think we should do this." I told him

"Do what?"

"Get back together. You're going to hurt me again, I know that. You always do." I reached for the roses and he handed them to me without a word. I smelled the roses and they smelled fresh. "Thanks for the flowers, that was nice of you, and I accept your apology, but I think it's time for you to leave." He remained silent. "Say something."

"You're not going to get rid of me that easily." He closed the space between us and got down on his knees in front of me. "You want me and I want you. It's that simple."

"No, it's" He cut me off with his lips and I couldn't help it, I kissed him back. His lips were soft and yummy. His tongue felt like home as it wormed around in my mouth. I was unaware of my body moving, but my legs must have opened because his body was pressed firmly against mine and his hands were rubbing up and down my back. My arms were hooked under his armpits and my hands were pulling down on his shoulders keeping him close to me. I couldn't deny how I felt. I couldn't explain it. I needed to love him the same way I needed air to breathe. I hungered for him and I couldn't imagine a future without his luscious lips in it. I had it bad. I felt some wetness sliding down my chin and I wondered if I was crying. I opened my eyes and broke the kiss. I smiled when I realized that it wasn't me. It was him. He was crying.

He leaned his forehead against mine and peered deep in to my soul as he said, "I love you."

I wanted to tell him I loved him, too, but something inside me made me hold back. "I know you do."

"Come home with me." He looked like he needed me as much as I needed him.

I opened my mouth to tell him no, but my voice had a mind of its own and a weak, "Yes" came out instead. He smiled as he moved back a little to give me a little breathing room. Something hit the floor. We both looked down and I almost died from laughter when I saw the squished bouquet of roses.

"There's that smile I love so much," he said as he traced his finger across my bottom lip. It tickled a little, making me smile even more. I felt giddy. I knew it was a golden moment. I snapped a picture in my mind and said a prayer that I would remember that moment forever because it was perfect.

He stood and held out his hand for me. I took it and I stood next to him. I didn't expect it, but he pulled me in to a hug. "I know nothing is settled, and I know we still need to talk about a few things, but let's wait until tomorrow because right now feels too good to mess up with words." His whispering voice sent hot air in to my ear and I felt like passing out from pure excitement when he kissed my ear and gave it a lick with his tongue. He was right about two things: I wanted him and the moment was too good.

I pushed away from him and said, "Let me say goodbye to Michael and grab my stuff."

"Okay, but don't be gone long." He gave me a peck on the lips. I turned and walked to Michael's bedroom door. When I got to the door, I turned to look at Lionel and he was staring at me with the most adorable smile on his face. My heart was warm and full.

I knocked on Michael's door and he opened it. He had some jazz playing really low.

He looked at the smile on my face and said, "I take it you're leaving." I giggled and shook my head then I laughed at myself for giggling. "My how your mood has changed," Michael teased as I walked in his room to get my stuff.

He was right, I had done a complete 180. Less than thirty minutes had passed since I was upset with Lionel, and I was acting like all was forgotten. Such was the way with love, I guessed.

I grabbed my bag and thanked him for being there for me. "That's what friends are for. You don't have to thank me because you know you're always welcome here. Now get your shit and get out." His smile and joking tone let me know that he was messing with me. I smiled at him before I turned to walk out.

Lionel and I walked down the hallway, out of the building and up to the bus stop with Lionel's arm around my shoulder. Our closeness should have made it obvious that we were more than friends. We got to our dorm room and we settled for spooning in my bed.

The next day, Lionel went with me to the health clinic. The results confirmed that I had Chlamydia, well a Chlamydia infection in the rectum to be exact. Talk about being uncomfortable in the doctor's office. It was embarrassing. The doctor gave me a choice of a single dose of azithromycin or a week of doxycycline, taking it twice daily. I picked the azithromycin. I had to go back in and get tested later to make sure I was clear and I was, so it was time to celebrate with Lionel.

There was only one thing I had on my mind. You would think getting a STD from him would slow me down, but I couldn't stop myself. I wanted to feel that big black dick inside me again. I physically ached to have him fuck me. The all clear from the doctor was like an early Christmas present. Lionel and I had a home game that night. He started and I came off the bench, but it was all good. Our team won, he was the leading scorer, and I had the most assists. I couldn't complain.

We went to the basketball after party at a nearby house. It was fun. We were drinking and joking around with the guys from the team and dancing with a bunch of fine ass girls, which only served to make me hornier. I was dancing with this one girl and she was grinding up on me something fierce. I mean damn! Her ass was soft and big and she knew how to work it as she took my dick to places I didn't know it could go on the dance floor. I finally reached a point when I couldn't take anymore. I was hard as a rock. I excused myself and went to find Lionel. I found him in the kitchen drinking a beer and talking to some chick. I walked over to him and grabbed his arm. "We need to go." I told him.

"Give me a sec." he said.

"We need to go now!" I told him as I pulled his arm. He looked in my eyes and I swear he understood what I meant. He almost killed himself trying to get out the chair. He jumped up so fast you would have sworn someone lit a fire under his ass.

He turned to the girl and said, "Sorry, babe, but I gotta go." He didn't even wait for her response. We were gone in a flash. We raced to our dorm. The elevators were on the 10th floor and there was no time to wait. We went running up the stairs and Lionel tripped over his own feet and fell when we were almost to our floor. I had to laugh.

He jumped up and said, "Keep laughing."

"I'm sorry. Are you okay?" I managed to ask between laughs. I was standing at the top of the flight of stairs so he walked up to me.

He leaned towards my ear and said, "You might want to save your energy because I'm going to wear your ass out." The laugh was followed by a little smile and then I just stood there as he ran up the next flight. "Come on!" I heard him shout from the top of the stairs.

I ran behind him and when we reached our floor, we burst through the door and almost knocked over a group of girls. Lionel had his keys in his hand and he opened our door and we both ran inside. He closed the door, locked it, and walked to his computer. He had his back turned to me as he made a playlist, so I kicked off my shoes, ripped my clothes off, hopped on his bed, and waited for him to catch up. "Hurry up," I told him.

He turned to look at me and had to do a double take when he saw that I was naked. "You're so romantic," he said.

"I know," I said with a smile on my face. His eyes worked their way down my body before focusing on my hardon. He licked his lips. He pushed the power button on his speaker and music came blaring out. The sound of rap filled the room. I wished it was some smooth love making music like R&B, but two guys locked in a room listening to sex songs probably wouldn't go over too well for our cover. The rap music was good enough though, because he picked ones that had good hard beats and lyrics that made you want to fuck something.

He took off his clothes and shoes and walked his naked chocolate ass over to me. I was leaking with anticipation. He leaned his face towards mine and stopped just short of contact. I moved my head up so I could kiss him. He pulled his head away, teasing me. I grabbed the back of his head with my right hand. Our lips touched and I felt a tingle shoot though my whole body. Our kiss became more passionate and just when I thought I would cum from kissing him, he pulled back. He leaned forward and whispered in my ear, "Let's do this right." He nicked my ear with his teeth. I forgot how much I liked that. He was still standing, so he jumped in bed next to me and proceeded to gently trace his fingers over the front of my body. Each touch was electric. By the time he worked his way to touching my dick, I had to stop him because I was afraid I would cum. He leaned over and blew hot air in my ear and whispered, "Go ahead and cum, you'll last longer when you fuck me." I was about to shoot right then. The thought of fucking him was pushing me over the edge. He started blowing hot air all over my neck before he sucked on it a little, then he blew hot air over my left nipple and attacked it like a rabid dog. He was sucking on it with such force that for a second I thought he might get some milk out of it. I felt the back of his hand slide down my stomach and then, he opened his hand and wrapped it around my dick. Two pumps and I was gone. I came with a grunt. I looked in his eyes and they were smiling back at me. Damn, he was good.

He gave me a few seconds to calm down before he climbed on top of me and started kissing me. His big dick was stabbing at my flesh, begging to enter somewhere. "Fuck me." I told him. He didn't need much convincing. He took his fingers and started warming me up for the real thing. When he thought I was ready, he got some more lube and a condom. I thought the condom was ironic. When I didn't know what he had, I let him do me without a condom, but when I knew he was clean, he was using a condom. I watched him put the condom on and line up at my entrance.

"You sure about this?" he asked.

"Fuck yeah," I told him. Seconds later he was pushing his way inside me. I thought I shot fast, but damn, he barely lasted three minutes. He came much faster than the first time.

"Sorry," he said as he rolled off of me.

"It's okay," I assured him.

"I was thinking about you fucking me and it was too much for me I guess. I didn't know you had such an effect on me," he gave me a small smile as he pulled me close to him so we could cuddle for a few minutes. About five minutes later, he said, "So, you ready for your turn?" He had a mischievous grin on his face.

"You mean it?" I asked him.

"Yes, now fuck me." He laughed.

"I hope I'm as good as you."

"Anything you do will be great. Just be gentle, because I'm a virgin." We both started laughing hysterically. It sounded so wrong for him to say he was a virgin, because he was far from that. He was a male slut, but technically he was a virgin to what I was about to do to him. I was about to make him mine in the same way that he made me his. Once he gave himself to me, we would be equal in our relationship.

I was surprised to find that I was still hard. I tried to follow the same techniques he used on me, thinking that he must like them. I bit his nipple and he let out the most erotic moan I had ever heard. I warmed him up with my fingers before preparing for my first ever male fuck. In a sense, we were both losing our virginity. I put on a condom after I lubed him up and I fucked him for twenty minutes while he moaned beneath me. I felt him stiffen up and he came, causing me to cum as his ass muscles contracted. I rolled to the side and we both stopped to catch our breath.

"I love you," he said.

"I love you, too," I said.

"That was good, but don't get any ideas. I'm not a bottom," he told me with a smile. We both laughed and I snuggled in his arms. The music was still playing in the background and I hoped that he didn't have the playlist on repeat. That was the last thought I had before I fell asleep in his arms, content with a night of passionate love making.

Chapter 11

Open up

The semester was over, the grades were in, and we were preparing to go home for Christmas. I was snuggled in his arms thinking about the journey home and our relationship. We were just going to be "friends" when we got off the bus and returned to our old routines for a few days, before heading back to school for practice and our next game. Thanksgiving was easy because we had a game that weekend and too much homework, so we couldn't go home, but now we had one game and nothing but time. My mind began to wonder and I started thinking about the talk we never had and that's when I was struck by an epiphany about us. Suddenly it was clear to me that we were trying to use a band-aid on a wound that wouldn't stop bleeding. Sure, the band-aid covered the bleeding and for a few moments it seemed okay, but then the blood soaked through the band-aid again and it was time for a new one. That's what sex was for us: a band-aid. After that night at Michael's, Lionel and I kissed and made out when we should have been talking. It was easier for us and I didn't complain, because I needed the closeness while I was dealing with the STD situation, and I really wanted the intimacy after I was clean, but the honeymoon was over and the delusions were dissipating. I realized our last few weeks together hadn't been peaches and cream and that I had overlooked his mistakes and shook them off as nothing.

I felt him nuzzle my neck with his nose and I knew he was waking up. He pulled me closer and his dick pressed against my ass as if it belonged there. Without thinking, I raised my thigh a little and he pushed his hard dick between my thighs. I closed my thighs and relaxed with the feeling of him between them. I didn't mean to do anything sexual but it seemed that was all we were good for. He started going in and out and moaning. I squeezed my thighs together harder when he tried to pull out because I knew he liked that. After a couple seconds, I started wondering what the hell I was doing. I felt like 'here we go again' and I didn't want to go there right then. I jumped out of the bed, grabbed my boxers off the floor and put them on.

"What the hell are you doing?" he asked.

"Putting my clothes on. What does it look like I'm doing?" I knew I didn't say it nicely.

"What the fuck is your problem?" he asked as he sat up in bed.

"That's all we do!" I yelled at him.

"What? And lower your voice, someone might hear you."

"No, I'm not going to lower my voice! There are only three damn people left on the whole fucking floor and I don't think Henry cares and frankly, I could give a flying fuck who hears me! All we do is have sex! We don't talk about anything." I could feel the frustration building in my body.

"We talk all the time!"

"Yeah, like what do you want for dinner, but we never talk about anything real! What about your lying, or the way you treat me, or the way you talk to me like trash sometimes? What about the way you scare me sometimes? What about the fact that you don't trust me? If you see me talking to a guy you don't know, you assume I'm sleeping with him or something, but we don't talk about it. We just kiss and make out like nothing's wrong, but something is very wrong! The past few weeks have been great physically, but we're just pretending to be happy and I'm tired of it! We need to talk!"

"Wah, wah, wah! You sound like a fucking baby! A whiny baby at that! Why don't you stop bitching and get back in bed!" I could see the anger rising in his eyes.

"No! I'm not getting back in bed until we talk!" I crossed my arms over my chest.

He threw the covers back and jumped off the bed. He lowered his face to mine, nose to nose, so to speak. "What the fuck do you want from me? I love you! You know that! Now get back in bed and we'll talk about this later." His look softened a little, "I promise."

"No." The anger returned to his face and in an instant, he had grabbed my arm and flung me on the bed with such force that the back of my head hit the wall and it hurt like hell. It took me a second to overcome the shock. Once I regained my composure, I looked at him. "What are you going to do? Take it?" He didn't say anything. I started pulling off my boxers. "Fine then, do it! That's all I'm good for to you anyway, so just do it!"

He didn't look angry anymore. There was a look of remorse on his face. "I'm sorry, baby, I didn't mean it." He came towards me and lifted his hand. I flinched. "Relax, I'm not going to hurt you." He rubbed my cheek and I wondered why everything seemed so familiar.

Finally, I pushed his hand away. "What's wrong with you?" I asked him.

His look changed from remorse to pure sadness. He started backing away from me and he sat down on his bed. "I'm sorry," he said as he put his head in his hands and sobbed.

I didn't understand him sometimes. I watched him cry for a few minutes and then my heart started to ache for him because I could feel his sadness. I got up, pulled my boxers up properly and walked over to him. I put my arms around him and he cried on my chest. I rubbed my fingers lightly over his head and said, "Ssh, ssh. It's okay."

"It's not okay," he said into my chest. The vibrations from his voice tickled across the few chest hairs I had. I knew there was something going on with him, and I was sick of not knowing. How could I help him if I didn't know what was wrong? I released my embrace as I sat next to him. I pulled his head back to my chest and he cried a little more. His crying slowly started to ease and soon all I heard was a few sniffles. "I don't want to be like them," he whispered.

"Like who?" I asked as softly as possible.

He was silent for a long time before he said, "Nothing."

"You don't have to be afraid to tell me anything. I won't judge you." I wasn't sure what to say to him, but that seemed like the best thing.

"I can't tell you," he whispered.

"Fine, you don't have to tell me right now." I pulled back from him and held his face up so I could look in his eyes. "But I hope you feel comfortable enough to tell me one day, because I love you, so your demons are my demons. Okay?"

He nodded but he remained silent. I gave him a peck on his lips and I stood up. He immediately grabbed me, "Don't go," he begged.

"I'm not going anywhere, I was standing up so you could stretch out on the bed and I could lie down next to you."

"Oh, okay." He stretched out on his bed and grabbed my hand. "Lie down on top of me please, so I can hold you." He sounded almost childlike when he said it.

I looked at his still exposed albeit soft penis and said, "I don't think that's such a good idea."

"It's okay, I won't try anything. I just want to hold you."

"You can hold me while I'm next to you." I pointed out.

"But it's not the same."

Usually I would have continued to argue with him, but the look on his face told me he didn't need sex right then. He needed me. "Okay." I got on top of him and rested my head on his chest. He put his arms around me and squeezed me tight. Nothing I wanted to talk about was important enough to try to discuss right then. I relaxed in his arms and let his heart lull me in to a trance like state. My mind stopped racing and I was able to focus my thoughts on the situation at hand. What started as a confrontation had ended as something even more confusing. I always suspected there was something he wasn't telling me. Finally, I knew for sure. I knew it was someone, and not something, that he was keeping secret. Someone was hiding in his memories, tormenting him. I was fairly certain I knew what part of the secret was, but I couldn't help but wonder if there was more.

"Are you asleep?" I heard a faint voice ask.

"Almost." I paused for a second. "I should probably roll off of you now because I know you don't want to wake up with my dead weight on top of you."

His grip tightened again. "I couldn't imagine waking up in a better predicament." He kissed the top of my head. "Besides, you know I can push your bony ass off me." He laughed and I swear I heard his laughter transform in to a smile on his face. I wanted to look at him, but I was too sleepy to move my head.

I fell asleep. My next memory was waking up still pressed against his body, with his hardon poking me, and wetness around my lips. I leaned my head up and brought my hand over to wipe away my drool. I looked at his chest and saw a small spot of wetness there. I don't know why I did it, but I couldn't help myself, I stuck my tongue out and licked the spot. I heard a moan escape from Lionel and that's when I realized his hands were inside my boxers and parked on my ass.

"You better stop that unless you want trouble," he joked.

I looked at him and was greeted by his beautiful, smiling face. "Feel better?" I asked.

"Yes, thank you," he said as his smile continued to brighten the room.

Seeing that he was in a good mood put me in a good mood and I smiled back at him until the urge to pee hit me. "I have to pee, so would you kindly unhand my ass?" He laughed.

"Sorry, my bad." He started pulling his hands out, but he couldn't just pull them out, he had to squeeze my ass a few times and slowly glide his hands up to my lower back.

I got off of him and said, "I think I'm going to take a shower while I'm in there."

"Sounds tempting."

"It shouldn't. I'm showering alone." I told him as I grabbed my robe and my shower stuff.

"You're such a tease!" he joked as I opened the door. I stopped and sat my robe and my shower stuff on my computer desk. I bent forward and lowered the back of my boxers. I moved my ass from side to side for a few seconds and I was about to pull up my boxers when I heard Lionel's bed creak. Sometimes I forgot how fast he was. He had his hard dick pressed against my ass in no time. I let out an involuntary gasp as I felt him behind me. I immediately stood up straight.

"Not now." I told him.

"I know. I just wanted to feel you so I could have something to think about." He slapped my left ass cheek and jokingly said, "Now get that ass in the shower before I want to do more than feel."

I pulled up my boxers, grabbed my things and was just about to close the door behind me when I felt the urge to look at him. I turned around and saw him standing there, naked, watching me. "I'll be back in a few minutes, okay?"

"I know you will," was all he said before I tore myself away from his smiling eyes and closed the door.

My shower was interesting. All the thoughts that had been racing around in my head returned and quickly resumed competition. I was thinking about so many different things, but all of them involved the same two constants, me and Lionel. I thought about the talk we still hadn't had and I wondered if we'd ever have it. Somehow I feared we wouldn't. Talking was obviously not a strong suit for either of us and I couldn't think of a good reason to bring the conversation up anytime soon. Lionel obviously had some issues he needed to work through and I wanted to be there for him, no questions asked and no drama given. My insecurities could wait until after I knew his situation.

I washed my hair in the shower and wondered if my mother would like my new haircut. I wondered if I should finally tell her that Lionel and I were together, or if I should continue to hide it from her in fear of her telling someone else. I knew Lionel would never tell his mother but he didn't talk much about his family, so I couldn't figure out if it was because his mother hated homosexuals, or if it was because he didn't have much to say about her.

I finished my shower and returned to find Lionel on his bed, stroking his dick. His eyes were closed and he was moaning my name repeatedly. "Lucas, yeah Lucas, suck that shit. Oh, oh, ohhh, I'm about to cum!"

I was tempted to say something and ruin his moment, but I thought better of it and instead lightly closed the door behind me and tiptoed over to him. I started rubbing my fingers up and down his chest and his eyes shot open as he looked to see who was touching him. He saw my face and smiled before continuing to stroke. I reached down and grabbed the hand that was wrapped around his dick. "Let me help you." I said as seductively as possible.

"You don't have to," he said between heavy breathing.

"I want to," I told him before I lowered my head and opened my mouth to suck his dick. I still couldn't take all of it, but I was getting better. He came a few seconds later and I swallowed. As I was swallowing his cum, I had one thought: I guess we're back to sex again.

"Thanks," he said as I lifted my head.

"You needed it," I told him without batting an eye. He got up, put a pair of boxers on, grabbed his shower stuff and dashed out the door and down the hallway. I was stupefied by his quick exit. I waited a few minutes before I decided to check on him. I walked in the bathroom and I heard him wailing in the shower. I wanted to go in and kiss wherever it hurt so I could take away his pain, but I knew there was nothing I could do unless he reached out to me. I stood there for a few minutes before the sound of his sniffles became too much for me. A brief moment of hesitation hit me as I turned to leave, but I swept it under the rug and walked back to our room.

Chapter 12

You Don't Want to Know

I sat in the window seat on the bus, looking out at the sun setting in the distance. Lionel was sitting next to me, with his head resting on my shoulder. I looked at the divider between our seats and smiled as I thought of how Lionel behaved when we first got on the bus. As soon as we sat down, Lionel pulled down the armrest and winked at me. He was very careful about how we interacted with each other in public, but I was sure anyone with half a brain could see the way we looked at each other and know that we must be more than friends. I liked to think that Lionel and I had that type of chemistry.

I saw the sign for our town limits and I almost wanted to cry because I knew we were going back to being Lucas and Jay again. The bus came to a stop as we pulled in to a parking space in the terminal. The bus driver announced the transfers and turned on the lights. I nudged Lionel. For a brief second, he forgot where we were; he leaned in and gave me a light peck on my lips, and I let him. He jerked away as he realized where we were. He looked around quickly to see if anyone was watching, but everyone was too busy doing their own thing to pay attention to us. He flashed me a half smile and stood to get his carry-on bag. I got up without thinking and hit my head. It was easy to forget that I couldn't stand straight up, when the person right next to me could. Lionel laughed at me.

"Great move, Einstein" he joked.

"No shit, Sherlock." I said.

He smiled at me. "What?" Then he laughed to himself and handed me my carry-on bag. We had the brilliant idea to throw our clothes in our gym bags since we weren't going to be home that long. We stepped off the bus and walked in the building. My parents were waiting for me.

"There's your fam," said Lionel as he pointed to our left.

My mother came running towards us. "Lucas!" she shouted as she hugged me and planted kisses on my cheek.

I pushed her off, blushing from the embarrassment of having her kiss me in front of Lionel, even though he had seen her kiss me several times before. "Mom!"

"Oh, sorry baby, I wasn't trying to embarrass you." She stepped back and pinched my cheek. I quickly pushed her hand away. "Oh, I'm so happy to see you. I missed you so much." The love in her eyes made me sad that I had pushed her away. She reached out and grabbed my hand, as she turned her attention to Lionel. "So how have you been? Has Lucas been treating you right? Are you okay, you look sick?"

I looked over at Lionel and was shocked to find that she was right, he did look sick. A few seconds before he looked fine, but he suddenly looked like he would throw up at any moment. "Are you okay?" I asked him as I put my arm around him.

"I'm fine!" he said, a little too emphatically for my taste, but that was not the time to question him.

My mother seemed to sense the tension because she said, "Well I'm happy Lucas has a friend to keep him company up there." Then she turned her attention to me and said, "Sweetie, why don't you go over there and say hello to your father while I talk to Lionel."

"Yes, Momma." I started walking towards my father. My father was standing with his usual uninterested look on his face. I could tell he wasn't too happy to see me. I walked up to him. "Hi Dad."

"Hey, son." He looked towards my mother and Lionel. I turned to look too because I was curious about what was going on. My mother was hugging Lionel and he looked like he was crying.

"What did she say to him?" I asked my father.

"Hell if I know." He grabbed my arm which made me turn and look at him. "Are you messing around with that boy?"

"Huh?" I could feel the panic building inside me. I never wanted to talk about things like that with him. "Why would you ask that?"

"I'm not stupid! There's something about the way the two of you looked as you were walking next to each other. You look too close to be just friends. Your mother noticed it the second she saw you. 'Looks like Lucas has a boyfriend,' she said before she ran to give you a hug." He looked me in my eyes. "She was right, wasn't she? You've turned that boy in to a faggot just like you?" I would like to say I was shocked and hurt by his words, but he had said much worse to me before.

"I didn't turn him in to anything!" I told him.

He glared at me and I knew he wanted to say something else, but he didn't. His eyes went back to my mother and Lionel. "What the hell is she doing?" he asked out loud.

I turned around and saw my mother planting kisses all over Lionel's face. It looked like she was kissing away his tears and I knew it was perfectly innocent, but part of me was jealous because I wanted to be the one kissing away his tears. I took my arm away from my father and went over to see what was going on with Lionel. He saw me approaching before I could get to them. He lightly pushed my mother away and tried to clean his face with his shirt. "What's wrong?" I asked.

My mother walked towards my father and Lionel stood still for a couple of seconds. I watched as the tears began to fall again. "She knows about us."

"I didn't tell her, Lionel. I swear."

"I know you didn't. She said she saw it the second we got off the bus. Are we that obvious?"

"I don't think so," I said as I reached for him. I hated lying to him, but I knew he couldn't handle the truth.

He jumped back and yelled, "Don't touch me!" drawing the attention of a few people in the terminal. "I can't be near you! I just can't! Not here!" He started walking towards one of the exits.

He got a nice head start before I realized I should be chasing him. "Wait!" I screamed as I ran after him.

He stopped and turned around. "Leave me alone! I will talk to you when we get back to school."

"Oh, so you're not going to talk to me on the bus ride back?" I asked as I reached him.

"You know what I mean."

"No, I don't!" I said. I dropped my gym bag, which was starting to press in to my arm the wrong way. "Why don't you tell me what you mean?" I whispered.

"I can't do this here. I mean, us, here. I can't do that. So please just stay away from me," he said in a low voice.

"Are you breaking up with me?"

"No. I just can't be with you while we're here."

"But I thought we were going to hang out?"

"How can we, when everyone is going to be able to see that something is going on between us?"

"But, I thought"

"Well, you thought wrong," he said cutting me off.

"We don't have to hang out with our friends, we can just hang out with each other."

"No."

"Why didn't you tell me this before we got here?"

"I wasn't sure. I had to see how it felt to be here with you. I don't know how to act like you're just my friend. At school, people accept our closeness because they think I'm trying to kiss your ass because I hit you with the ball that day, but here, it's different. These people know I don't kiss anybody's ass and they'll see how I treat you and they'll know something's going on."

"You're being paranoid." I told him.

"Your mother took one look at us and she knew. I don't want that thought to cross anyone else's mind."

"My mother knows about me, of course she would jump to that conclusion, but that doesn't mean other people will notice." I took a breath and said, "We should talk about this."

He smiled. "You always want to talk, but there's nothing to talk about. I've told you everything I have to say, so relax, we're still together and I'll see you when we get ready to board the bus back to our place." Then he did something that melted my heart. He lifted two of his fingers to his lips and kissed them, then he looked around and when he realized no one was looking, he put his fingers on my lips like a flash and then it was over. I knew it was nothing, but to me it felt like everything. He was afraid that he loved me too much to act like his old self around me, at least that's what I heard.

"Okay," I said. He pulled me in to a hug and squeezed me.

"I'm going to miss you," he whispered. He let go of me and turned to walk away.

I grabbed his arm to stop him. "Let us drop you off at home."

He turned his head to look at me. "It's easier this way."

I let go of him and he walked away. As he walked out the door, I felt a hand on my shoulder. I glanced over and saw my mother. "It's okay Sweetie, he'll come around." All the anger I thought I should be feeling towards Lionel, was directed squarely at my mother.

I moved away from her touch. "What did you say to him? You chased him away!" I told her.

"Don't be upset. I told him that I could tell he really cared about you then he fell apart and started crying. You know how I am; I had to try to comfort him. I told him that his secret was safe with me."

"You scared him! He doesn't want people to know and you told him that you could tell just by seeing us! How could you do that?"

"Honey, calm down. I wasn't trying to upset him." She put her arm around me. "Now why don't you tell me what happened?"

I wanted to be a brat; I wanted to pull away from her again, but I needed her comfort, so I let her pull me close. "He doesn't want to talk to me while we're here. He's afraid everyone will see us together and know that something is going on."

"Oh, baby, I'm sorry. I'm so sorry," she said. Her other arm came around to embrace me and I cried on her shoulder.

A voice whispered, "Would you stop that! You look like a damn fairy!"

My mother pulled away from me. "Don't talk to him like that!" she yelled at my father.

"It's bad enough he is what he is, but now he's got that boy confused and he's standing here crying on your shoulder. I can tolerate what he is, but I don't need him rubbing it in my face." He grabbed my bag and then grabbed my arm. "Come on. Let's go home." There were only a few people in the terminal, but the way my father acted, you would have thought there were a lot more. He kept his grasp on my arm until we reached the car. He dropped my bag on the ground as he opened the car door. He pressed the button to unlock the other doors and said, "Get in!" I grabbed my bag and got in.

As we were leaving the parking lot, I looked over and saw Lionel waiting at the local bus stop. We made eye contact and I smiled at him. He smiled back and I knew we would work it out. My parents had a huge fight on the way home. My mother was telling my father that he shouldn't call me a fag or a fairy because it wasn't nice, and my father was telling my mother that as long as I was his son, he would call me whatever he damn well pleased. I tuned them out by thinking about Lionel. I wanted to do something special for him, so I decided I would take his Christmas present to his house. I realized that I had never been inside his house. I always knocked on the door, or blew my horn, and he would come out and we would go about our business. I wondered what he was hiding. I hadn't thought about it before, but knowing how messed up he was on the inside, I wondered if the demon lived with him, and if he was afraid that by letting me in, he would somehow let the demon out. We pulled in to my driveway as I made the decision to try to get inside Lionel's house.

That night was uneventful besides the talk I had with my father in the kitchen around two in the morning. I couldn't sleep, so I went to the kitchen to get some milk and cookies, and my father came downstairs. He sat and talked for almost an hour. He apologized for the way he acted and explained that it was a shock for him to think about me with a boyfriend, but he still shouldn't have called me those names. I accepted his apology, as I always did. I went back to bed and tried to sleep. I missed having Lionel cuddled up against to me. I missed our beds at school. I missed our blankets. I missed the warmth that I felt when he was near me. My bed at home felt cold and empty and I felt alone.

Christmas went by without a hitch. I gave my parents their presents and they gave me some money and some clothes. I hadn't spoken to Lionel in two days, and I was ready to try to see him at his house. I knew I was risking him getting upset, but it was worth it just to see him, because I felt physically ill not being around him.

I told my parents I was going to visit some friends, but I think they knew exactly where I was going. I sat in my car in front of Lionel's house for ten minutes before I worked up the courage to get out. It felt strange to come to his house unannounced because I had always called when I was going to drop by. I got out the car with his present, all beautifully wrapped, and a card in my hand. I walked to the door and knocked.

"Who is it?" asked a young sounding voice.

"It's Lucas. I'm a friend of Lionel, um, I mean Jay." It was hard for me to call him Jay.

I heard the door unlock. A little boy stood there. I looked at him and he looked like a miniature Lionel. "Hello, is Jay home?" The little boy shook his head 'yes.'

He walked in the house and sat down on the floor in front of a television. I closed the door behind me. I stood there for a minute, observing a room I had never seen before. There wasn't much furniture. There were beer bottles all over the table and something that looked like drug paraphernalia, but I wasn't sure because I had never seen drug stuff anywhere other than on television and in the movies.

"So, where is he?" I asked the little boy.

"He's upstairs, but we can't bother him right now. You have to wait until he comes downstairs."

"I'm sure he won't mind," I said as I went to the stairs and started walking up.

"I wouldn't disturb them if I were you. You're going to get in trouble." The little boy warned from his seat on the floor.

"I'll be okay," I told him as I continued up the stairs. My heart was racing as I prepared myself to see Lionel and whoever it was he was with up there.

When I reached the top of the stairs, I heard a woman moaning. "Oh, shit! Oh, Jay! Make me happy Jay! Yeah, that's it!"

I should have turned around then, but I couldn't. I had to see for myself what was going on in the room. I stood outside the closed door and listened before I tried to twist the knob.

"Oh, Jay, put it in baby! Put it in! I need it! Oooohh! You're so big, baby! Just like your Daddy!"

I couldn't listen anymore. I tried to turn the knob, and to both my horror and my shock, the knob turned. I pushed the door open and the scene before me made me wish I was blind. I dropped the present. "That's just sick!" I shouted.

Lionel looked over at me. His eyes were bloodshot and they moved like they couldn't really focus on me. "Lucas?" he asked in a childish voice. "How'd you get over there?" He looked down at the woman below him. "You said you were Lucas," he said to her. His words were slurred. He turned to me. "Lucas?"

The woman turned his head back to her. "Ssh. I'm Lucas, baby. I'm Lucas." She pulled him in to a kiss. They continued what they were doing as if I wasn't there.

I tried to keep it in, but that sight pushed my stomach over the edge. I started vomiting, mostly on top of the present. I turned and ran out of there as quickly as I could. I flew out the front door, slamming it shut behind me. I got in my car. I wiped my lips and screamed. I started banging on the wheel, trying to release some of the agony I felt. I finally settled for placing my head in my hands and sobbing until my body physically couldn't make any more tears.

Some secrets were better left as secrets.

Chapter 13

No Words

I'm not sure how long it took for the tears to stop falling, but at some point, I looked in the mirror and saw my puffy eyes and my red face. I looked about as horrible as I felt. My mind was a flurry of thoughts, constantly racing back to that awful image. I wondered if I should go in the house and grab the little boy, to save him from that place. No child should have to grow up in a house like that. I wondered if I should go in and grab Lionel and save him from that woman. I knew I could take her. What she was doing was wrong, not to mention sick. Then I had another thought, 'This probably wasn't the first time.' I slapped myself hard in the face as I covered my mouth and nose with my hand.

"Oh my God!" I screamed against my hand. "Oh my God! Oh, my God! Oh my God! Oh goodness! Oh my God!" I moved my hand and rubbed my fingers across my head before balling my hand in to a fist and tapping my forehead repeatedly. I felt like I was going crazy. "What's going on?" I asked myself out loud. "Oh! What's going on here? Why is this happening? Oh my goodness!" I realized I was having trouble breathing, so I tried to take deep breaths. I started hyperventilating, which scared me. I closed my eyes and put my head back against my seat. I focused on my breathing, which seemed to make it worse at first, because it was like my brain was fighting my body, but after a few minutes, the pace of my breathing slowed down. I needed to get away from that place. I put my key in the ignition, started the car, and tore off down the street. I was in no condition to drive, but I had to get away. I pulled in my driveway and sat there while I gathered myself. Unfortunately, my time was cut short because my father came out to take some trash to the backyard. He was on his way back before he saw me. He walked over to my window and I rolled it down.

"Are you okay? You look like Hell! Did that boy dump you?" He said it all in one breath.

"Just leave me alone please. I'll be inside in a minute."

"Well, don't stay out here all damn day, pouting."

I slammed my hands against the steering wheel. "Dad, will you just leave me alone? I promise I'll only be out here for a few minutes."

"Don't take that tone with me! I'm still your father! But I can tell you're hurting right now, so I'll let that go." He leaned in through the window and pointed his finger at me. "You better check your attitude at the door!"

'Just what I need,' I thought. I pushed the button and rolled the window back up. 'Might as well get this over with,' I told myself as I took out the key and opened my door. I had just shut the car door, when I noticed something in the passenger seat. There was the card I bought for Lionel. I unlocked my door and reached across the seat to grab the card. I knew I had taken it in the house with me, but I didn't remember bringing it back to the car. I felt a tear slide down my face and I impulsively started ripping up the card. When I was done, there were little pieces strewn on the cold ground, resting on top of the light trace of snow. I slammed my door shut, and it created a breeze that forced some of the pieces to move.

Watching those pieces move away from me triggered something. I knelt down and feverishly started picking up the pieces of the card. I picked up the pieces that had fallen under my car and the few that were scattered in the flowerbed next to the driveway. I had a handful of pieces, when my eyes caught sight of two missing pieces towards the end of the driveway. I walked towards the pieces, and a gust of wind came by and snatched them away from me. I watched as the wind lifted the pieces off the ground and danced with them in the air, spinning them around. The wind died and the pieces fell in the middle of the street. I seemed to be moving in slow motion as I approached the sidewalk. It felt like an out of body experience, almost, like a dream. I took one step off the sidewalk and I was jarred back to reality by the sound of a horn as a car went zipping by me. I jumped and my hand twitched, throwing all the pieces in the air. 'Damn,' I thought.

I turned and walked towards the backyard. I opened the garage and grabbed the broom and dustpan that my father kept in there. I walked back to the street and waited for a few cars to pass then I swept the pieces in to the dustpan, gathering a mix of snow, dirt and little rocks along with the pieces. I only swept the big pieces, leaving the other ones to travel on their own. I didn't want all the pieces anymore. I just wanted to clean up the mess. I took the dustpan to the backyard and dumped its contents in the trashcan. I put the lid on the can. I wiped my face on my shirt and turned to go inside.

My mother was sitting in the kitchen waiting for me. "Your father told me you and Lionel broke up. Come here and tell me what happened." She stood and opened her arms and I was powerless to resist. I wanted to be her little boy again. I wanted her to kiss the wound and make the hurting stop. I fell in her arms and cried on her shoulder. I knew I was squeezing her too hard, but she didn't complain. She just put her arms around me and held me. "What happened?"

"I can't talk about it. God! I don't even want to think about it. Oh, Momma, it was bad. It was so bad." She didn't press me to tell her anything else. She just held me and let me cry.

"Oh, not again!" My father exclaimed as he walked in the kitchen. "You need to stop babying him!"

"Leave us alone!" My mother told him.

"I'm getting a snack then I'll be gone. I can't watch you do this to him!" he told her.

I loosened my grip on my mother and tried to pull away, but she held me tighter. "Ssh Baby, don't let him bother you. Pretend he's not there. He'll be gone soon."

I hugged her again but I stopped crying because I didn't want him to see me like that. I heard him pouring a drink and then I heard his footsteps as he walked away. My parents rarely argued, but they were severely separated on the issue of my sexuality. My mother had jumped on board right away, but my father was still swimming next to the boat, sometimes he kept up, but most of the time the boat was pulling away from him.

He was gone and she was holding me. "Are you going to be okay?" she asked.

"No."

"What can I do to help?"

"Nothing."

"You know I'm always here for you no matter what. Right?"

"I know."

"And you know you can talk to me about anything?"

"I know, but I can't talk to you about this. I don't know if I'll ever be able to talk to you about it."

"You need to talk about it."

"I can't."

"You'll feel better if you do," she told me as she rubbed her hand over my head.

"I can't."

"Okay, Baby. Okay." She rubbed her hand over my head a few more times. "I miss your hair," she said. "Why'd you cut it so short? It's like stubble on your head." She laughed, but I knew what she was doing.

"I just wanted to try something different. Lionel liked" I stopped mid sentence. I didn't want to talk about him. I didn't want to hear his name and I didn't want to think about him. "I'm going to go take a nap." I told her as I let go of her and walked down the hall.

"Okay," I heard her say.

When I reached my room, I kicked off my shoes, got in my bed, and tried to relax. I was the idiot who convinced Lionel that we should surprise our parents by staying two extra days. It only cost ten dollars to make the adjustment, and we would be back before our next game. At the last minute, Coach had cancelled practice for the days before the game and scheduled a team meeting on game day. He said we would go over a few plays and that would be it because we all deserved to go home and fully enjoy our holiday, without rushing back for practice. I think he was the one who wanted to fully enjoy his holiday, but who was I to complain.

Dumb ideas can be well thought out. That's what I had: a dumb idea. I knew things would be different when we went home, but I never expected so much to change. How could I look at him the same, knowing what I knew? If we had just come for one day and gone right back, it never would have happened. I started to wonder if maybe I was partly to blame. I was the one who changed the schedule. I cleared the way for things to happen. Then I realized that Lionel was a grown man. He might not have been in his right state of mind when I saw him, but he should have known better than to allow himself to get that far gone. I didn't know what to think. The quiet of my room only amplified the voices in my head. How could I deal with what I had witnessed?

I must have worried myself to sleep because I awoke to the sound of my mother calling my name. "Lucas!"

"Huh?" I responded.

"Dinner's ready."

"Okay, I'm coming." I forced myself to get out of bed and I went downstairs. My mother and father were already at the table. It would be our last meal together before I left again. I was dreading the idea of getting on the bus. I was afraid of seeing Lionel.

I sat down at the table and for forty minutes, everything returned to normal. We talked about my classes and some of my old high school friends. My mother told me how much she was going to miss me, and complained that I didn't come home for Thanksgiving. She told me if I didn't come home the next year, she was bringing Thanksgiving to me, wherever I was. Other than that, it was a normal dinner, with no talk of Lionel, or me being gay, or anything that might bring drama.

After dinner, my father asked what time I needed to be at the station in the morning and I told him 6 am. He frowned because he hated getting up before 7:30, but he shook his head and told me to be ready to leave by 4 am.

"For what?" I asked.

"You should always be early."

"Lionel and I got to the bus station thirty minutes before our bus left."

"Well, I don't care what you and Lionel did."

He said it in a way that insinuated he was referring to more than just the time we arrived at the station. I hated the venom in his voice when he said it, but most of all, I hated the subject. I wished I could clear my mind of all the thoughts I had about Lionel. "I'll be ready at 4," I told him. My submission must have caught him off guard, because he opened his mouth to say something, but he didn't say anything. He closed his mouth and shook his head and I took that as my dismissal.

I attempted to go to sleep again, but my mind was unable to rest. I got out of bed at 2 am and started packing my bag. 'I should have never tried to go to his house,' I thought. Things would be so different if I had just stayed home, but I wanted to surprise him before we left. I shouldn't have done that. I couldn't help thinking that what I saw was somehow my fault. The little boy told me not to go upstairs, but I didn't listen. I should have waited, or come back later, or anything. I shouldn't have opened that damn door. What was I really expecting to see? No matter who he was with, it still would have been something I didn't want to see. Hearing it was bad enough. Why did I open the door?

I kept having the same thoughts. One second I hated him, then I hated her, then I hated me. Everything was mixed up in my mind. A few times, I almost went to wake my mother and talk to her, but I knew I wouldn't be able to tell her in words what I had seen or how I was feeling. I had to somehow deal with it myself.

By 3:30, I was sitting on the sofa in the living room, waiting for my parents. My father came in around 3:45. He sat down in one of the chairs. "Your mother will be down in a minute," he told me. We sat there in silence for a few minutes. "You know you'll always be my son," he said out of the blue. I knew what he was really saying, 'Your mother and I were talking about the way I treat you. I just want you to know that no matter how much we argue, or disagree, I'll always love you.'

"I know, Dad. I love you, too." He glanced at me, and our eyes met. He quickly looked away. He reached for the remote that was on the table and turned on the television. He wanted to end the conversation, so I obliged. He loved me. That's why I always forgave him when he had one of his outbursts. I knew it was killing him that I wasn't normal.

My mother came down five minutes later with her coat on and her purse in hand. "You guys ready?" she asked. Neither of us answered. My father turned off the television and left the room. I put on my coat and grabbed my bag.

At 4:45, we were walking in the terminal. The terminal was desolate and reminded me of how I felt on the inside. I placed my bag in line at the door and went and talked with my parents. By 5:10, a few more people had drifted in. I saw some people I went to high school with so I went over and talked to them for a while. We caught up on the latest news, and I told them about some of the guys from the basketball team who I tracked down when I first got back. I let them know that everyone was fine. That's when this one girl, who I was told had a crush on me in high school, asked, "So how's your boy, Jay? I remember you two used to be pretty close. Where is he now anyway?"

"He's fine. He goes to my school."

"Really?" she asked. "I should have known you two would go to school together. That basketball team must me scary with both of you on it. You see him a lot?"

"He's my roommate."

"Oh, that's cool! I wish one of my girls would have gone to school with me and been my roommate, because the girl I'm living with now is a whack job." The other members in our crowd laughed.

I changed the topic and asked where they were headed. They told me they were headed to surprise one of my old teammates on the other side of the country who couldn't make the trip home for the holidays because he had practice and a game. I thought that was sweet of them, but I knew they were really just going to party. They told me they had a two hour bus ride and then they were catching a plane and flying out to see him. They said they were staying at a nice hotel that they all chipped in to pay for and they were going to go to his game and spend a few days with him, before they came back home and chilled for the rest of their break. I wished I could have a month break like them, but basketball players don't get winter break. I also wished I could have flown away with them, anywhere was better than where I was headed.

At 5:30, the first boarding call for my bus was made and I excused myself from my former classmates. I went over to my parents and said my goodbyes. To my surprise, my father hugged me and told me to come back soon. My mother hugged me and gave me a kiss on the cheek. I was happy that there weren't many people on the bus at 6. I knew we were going to stop and pick up more passengers along the way, but I liked having my own seat and my own space to do battle with my thoughts. I wondered where Lionel was, but I was relieved that I didn't have to face him. The bus driver got on the bus and I thought I was in the clear, but then he opened the bus door for someone. A few words were exchanged then Lionel walked on the bus.

Lionel looked disheveled. He had stubble on his face like he hadn't shaved the whole time he was away. His clothes were wrinkled and a mess. He was wearing sunglasses; his bag was half open, with clothes hanging out. I prayed he wouldn't see me, but I guess I should have known better. He walked directly to me, put his bag in the bin, and sat down next to me. I noticed he had a foul odor too, like he desperately needed a shower.

"What's up?" he asked as he assaulted my nose with his breath. I assumed he hadn't brushed his teeth either.

I wasn't sure what to say, or how to react. "Did you get my present?" I asked him. For some reason, the gift was the first thing that popped in my head. I think part of me wanted to know if he liked what I got him.

"What present?" he asked.

"Nothing, sorry, I'm a little confused."

"Oh, okay," he said.

I put my hand on his shoulder and he almost jumped out of his skin. I pretended like I didn't notice. "So how was your visit?" I asked. I wondered if he even remembered.

Chapter 14

Baring the Burden

The bus ride was not at all as I expected. For starters, I was afraid to mention Lionel's smell, so that made things a bit awkward. Lionel told me he didn't do much during the break and I did not have the heart to confront him with what I knew to be the truth of his time at home. Our conversation was strained, but we talked for a little while and he fell asleep with his head on my shoulder. I watched him sleeping and part of me felt like I should hold on to him and protect him from the horror that was his life. I guess that was the magic of love. I hadn't wanted to see him but after talking to him all I could think about was making everything better for him, but I knew there would be no kissing away the pain. He looked peaceful as he slept. I couldn't imagine what he was going through, but I promised myself that I would help him. I reached for his hand just to feel his skin. 'Still soft,' I said to myself as I traced my finger along the backside of his hand. I took my hand away, not wanting to draw any attention to myself. "Why can't this be easy?" I whispered.

I closed my eyes once to try to sleep, but the images of what I had seen wouldn't give me peace. I gave up on sleeping and wondered about Lionel and us and if it was really possible to help him. His damage was much more severe than I ever could have imagined. I wondered if a part of him knew the truth, but was blocking it out.

His situation broke my heart and boggled my mind. My heart cried out for me to help him; my brain told me the situation was too much for me to handle; so my eyes shed tears of confusion that I wiped away with my shirt. I gathered myself and sat there, burning a hole in to the top of his head. I stared at him until he woke up. He moved his head and looked at me. He took off his sunglasses.

"What's wrong?" he asked.

'Everything,' I thought. "Nothing," I said.

"You've been crying," he whispered.

"Just thinking. That's all."

"Thinking about what? Your fam? Did something happen while you were home?"

His question made me sigh. I wasn't the one something happened to. "No, it's not that. I don't know. I'm feeling emotional, I guess." I sent up a small prayer that he would drop it.

He scrunched his nose and sniffed the air. "Eww, what is that smell?" He smelled me, then he lifted his shirt and smelled it. "Eww!" he exclaimed as he let go of his shirt. "I stink. How can you sit next to me?"

"The smell started to fade after the first hour," I told him with a smile.

"You must really, well you know."

'Yeah,' I thought, 'I must really love you.' He got a devilish look on his face and I knew he was up to something. He reached for me and I pulled away, "Don't do it," I warned him, but there was no stopping him. He pulled my head in to his armpit and I had a big whiff of his funk. I'm not sure he realized exactly how ripe he was, but the smell made me want to vomit. He released me and I was gasping for air.

"It's not that bad is it?"

"Worse," I told him as I waved my hand in front of my nose, trying to drive away that awful smell. "Did you forget how to shower?" I joked. His expression changed and I instantly regretted saying anything, but he was the one who had brought it up.

"I woke up late," he said. His eyes had a sad look in them. He quickly put back on his glasses.

'He has to know something is wrong,' I thought. "Oh."

"Are we almost there?" he asked, changing the subject.

"I think so but I haven't been paying much attention." I suddenly didn't want to talk to him anymore. "I'm going to try to get some sleep."

"Okay."

I leaned my head against the window and closed my eyes. I saw those awful images again, so I had to weigh two options: suck it up and see the images, or open my eyes and look at Lionel. I decided to endure the images. I hated pretending I was sleep, but I feared looking in to his eyes. I felt him lean his head on my shoulder. I finally managed to fall asleep.

"Wake up," a voice said. I opened my eyes and became aware of Lionel's hand on my shoulder. "Wake up."

The bus came to a stop and the driver said something, but I wasn't paying attention. I was a little out of it as we got off the bus and walked to the local bus stop. We rode in silence on the city bus and neither of us spoke until we reached our room. "We're back," I said as I walked through the door.

"Yeah."

The room was exactly as we had left it, but nothing felt the same. Lionel excused himself to take a shower and I sat in the chair at my computer desk, thinking about him and her. A picture on his dresser caught my attention. They were both smiling in the picture and it looked perfect, but I knew it was all a lie, one big damn lie. I was so entranced by the picture that I did not notice Lionel return. He put his hand on my shoulder and scared the shit out of me. "Ahh," I screamed.

"It's only me. Relax." Lionel walked to his bed and sat down. "What's wrong with you?"

I looked at him and what I saw made me want to cry again. He had shaved and his brown skin was glistening. He only had on a towel. Usually I loved to see him half naked because he had a great body, but seeing him like that made me feel sick and I felt my stomach churning. His nakedness was repulsing me. I put my hand over my mouth. "I think I'm going to be sick."

He jumped off his bed and came over to me. He touched my forehead. "You feel sort of warm," he told me as I tried to shrink away from his touch.

I didn't want to feel that way around him and I didn't understand why I felt that way. I wanted to help him, I really did, but I kept seeing that image of him and her and I wasn't able to cope with it. Everything was too fresh, and I was starting to feel bipolar as my mind hurled between reaching out to him and running away from him. He reached to touch me again.

"Don't touch me." I told him as I pulled away.

"What the fuck is your problem?" I didn't answer him. He backed away from me. "Are you on that shit again?"

"What shit?"

"Niqua."

I honestly hadn't thought about that bitch since we left campus. "No, not that shit," I told him. He looked away. I waited for him to say something, but he didn't. He stood up and walked to his dresser. As he was rummaging through the middle drawer, I saw scratches on his back. "What happened to your back?" the cruel part of me asked, trying to somehow force a confession.

He turned around and looked at me. "You did it."

"No, I didn't."

"Yes you did!"

"When did I do it?" I challenged.

"I don't remember. You must have done it before we left."

"No, I definitely didn't do it. So if I didn't do it, who did?"

"What the fuck do you want from me?" he asked as he took off his towel and put on a pair of boxers. "I'm not cheating on you. You're the one who's always talking to strange guys!"

"You know I would never cheat on you! Don't try to turn this on me. Someone put those marks on your back," I told him. A tiny part of me felt guilty for pushing him, but I thought it was what he needed.

He stood in front of me and looked down in to my eyes. "Well I was at home the whole damn time, so if it wasn't you, who the hell do you think it was?"

"I don't know. Maybe someone you live with." I said.

He lived with her, so it was obvious what I was insinuating. He backhanded me and I fell out the chair, with the side of my face crashing against the floor. "Don't say that kind of shit!" he yelled.

I stood up and touched the liquid oozing from my lips. I held my hand up so I could confirm that the dripping stuff was in fact blood. His reaction had caught me off guard. I knew if I pushed him too far, he would lash out, but I wanted him to tell me. I had to hear him explain what was going on, although a tiny part of me thought I had no right to any explanation. I looked in his eyes, and he immediately averted his gaze, but he was too late. His eyes told me he was caught. "You remember, don't you?"

"Remember what?" he asked.

"What happened while you were at home? You know who put those marks on your back, don't you?"

The look in his eyes frightened me. I started backing away only to run in to my desk behind me. He began walking towards me and I feared what he might do. "What are you trying to say?" he asked.

His eyes pierced me, bursting my balloon and deflating the bravery I felt. "Nothing. I'm trying to say nothing. I'm just talking."

"You're not just talking." He grabbed my arms and squeezed them, but he was speechless for a few seconds. His grip was starting to hurt. I could feel my body shaking. "Why'd you do it?" he asked.

"Do what?"

"Come to see me."

"I thought you didn't remember that?"

"Ronnie told me you stopped by."

"So why did you pretend like you didn't remember?"

"I didn't want you to know how I lived."

"How long has she been doing that?" I asked, feeling a little braver.

"What?" His grip was still hurting me.

"I know what she did to you." I said.

He looked bewildered like I was speaking another language. He let go of me and backed away. "You don't know anything!" I reached out and put my hand on his shoulder. It was his turn to pull away. "Get away from me!" he screamed.

"I just want to help you," I told him.

"I don't need your help! You don't know shit!"

I thought our conversation was going to end with him admitting everything and telling me how she had been abusing him for years, but he had other plans. He retreated back in to his shell of denial. "It's okay, it's not your fault," I told him, trying to use the tactics I had seen on television.

"Just leave me alone!" He turned his back to me and walked to his dresser. He put on a pair of pants and a sweatshirt. "I'm going out," he said. I was still standing in the same spot. He left and I broke down. I fell to the floor and I cried. I was scared; I was confused; I was tired; I felt sick, and I was wondering if Lionel would be back. I hoped he wouldn't run away again.

The phone rang and I answered it, "Hello."

"Put Jay on the phone."

It was her. "He's not here."

"Where did he go?"

"I don't know."

"What the hell did you say to him?"

"Nothing."

"I know you said something. You couldn't keep your damn mouth shut, could you?"

"What you did was wrong."

"What happens in my house is none of your business."

"Lionel is my business, and I'm going to make sure that he never comes back to your house again!"

"So you would take him away from his son?"

"What? You had a child with him?" I suddenly felt woozy.

"No! He did that all by himself and left me to take care of the little bastard."

'Ronnie,' I thought, realizing why the little boy looked like a miniature Lionel. "I have to go."

"No you don't. What happened to the days when we used to chat?"

"Those days flew out the window when I saw you with him. Ugh. I don't even want to think about it." I wanted to hang up the phone, but I couldn't.

"Oh, thanks for the present," she said.

"I bought that for Lionel!" I told her.

"I know, but we share everything."

The sick emphasis she put on 'everything' was enough to bring me back from the haze my mind was in. Hearing that gave me the strength to hang up the phone. I couldn't believe her nerve, to call me and talk trash and rub her abuse of the man I loved in my face. I may not have wanted to sleep with him anytime soon, but I sure as hell didn't want her sleeping with him either. She was a sick person and he needed help to get away from her. I vowed I wouldn't let him down. My goal that night became to save him from her and from himself.

I tried to call Lionel to check on him, but he wouldn't answer the phone. I wanted to find him and love him; I wanted to swoop down like his guardian angel and save him. I wanted so many things and that night I didn't get any of them. I called Lionel all night, but he never answered his phone.

I breathed a sigh of relief when I heard the door unlock early the next morning. If I had known what was going to happen, I wouldn't have smiled when Lionel walked in.

Chapter 15

Fresh Bruises

I sat up. "Are you okay?" I asked after he shut the door.

"I'm fine!"

"Good, I was worried about you."

"Why?" He stepped further in to the room and I could smell the alcohol.

I grabbed my nose. "Did you bathe in it? Ugh!"

"I asked you a fucking question!" he shouted. "Why were you worried about me?"

I released my nose. "Because I love you." I thought he would calm down but telling him I loved him only served to change the expression on his face. The scowl was gone and a look of confusion took over. I stood up and he walked towards me. His face changed again and I saw tears in his eyes. I opened my arms and he fell in to them and I honestly believed everything was okay. He pushed me away and I fell on my bed.

"I hate you!"

'Not again,' was the first thought that entered in my head. "No you don't," I said as I stood up.

"Yes I do!" He threw a punch at my head, but the alcohol had him moving slowly so I was able to step out the way. That must have pissed him off because he attacked me with a flurry of punches.

His behavior upset me. I was trying to help him, and he was trying to beat me. My mind shut off for a minute and my reflexes took control. I hit him back and the fight was on. We ended up wrestling on the floor. At some point he had me pinned, with his forearm pressed against my neck.

"I need the room," he said.

"Huh?"

"I told Rachel I would call her when I got you out. I need the room."

"You what? Who?"

"I need to fuck someone."

My first thought was, 'You can fuck me.' "What?" I asked him, as my anger became that of a slighted lover. I wiggled my arm free from between us and reached up and slapped him across his face. "What?"

"Are you deaf? I'm having company, so get your shit and get out. I'm going to need some privacy!"

"Why are you doing this?" My anger was gone. All I felt was hurt and empty. I wanted to help him and he wanted to leave me. The tears fell like a waterfall.

"Because I hate you."

"You don't hate me! You love me! I know you do! You have to!"

He moved his forearm off my neck and put his hands next to my head like he was going to do a pushup. The fight was over. I wiped my eyes and looked up at him. He lowered his body on top of me and looked in my eyes. "I don't love you," he whispered. I knew he was trying to convince himself.

My head told me he didn't mean it, but I still felt the pain. My heart cracked a little. "Yes you do," I whispered back. I rolled us over so I was on top and I kissed him. He kissed me back. I broke the kiss and gently nibbled on his neck before whispering in his ear, "I know you love me." He didn't respond so I kept going. I worked my way down his body and I pulled down his pants and his boxers. I knew it was wrong but I wanted to make him happy and I wanted him to forget about Rachel, whoever she was. I put my lips around the tip of his dick and lowered my mouth. He moaned in pleasure. I sucked him for a few minutes before he pushed me off and changed our positions. He was on top of me, pushing his dick in and out of my mouth. It was okay at first, but somewhere in the middle, things changed. He picked up the pace and pushed deeper. He knew I couldn't take all of him, but he didn't seem to care. I gagged a few times as he forced his dick down my throat. By the end, he was fucking my mouth with such anger and force that my head was being banged on the floor each time he thrust in and out. He finally came, and I swallowed. He took his dick out of my mouth.

"Clean it," he demanded. I stuck out my tongue and did as he told me. When I was finished cleaning it, he stood and pulled his boxers and pants back up.

I stayed on the floor, feeling dirty and used. I watched as he grabbed a bag and put a few items of his clothes in it. "Where are you going?" I asked.

"Away from you. I can't stand to look at you!" He zipped up the bag, "You can have the damn room! We'll go somewhere else."

"What about the game?"

"I'll be there. Now stop talking to me."

"Why?" He ignored me and walked towards the door. "Why?" He walked out the door and slammed it shut. I was on the floor, crying. 'Why did he do this? How could he do this? Did I do this? Was it my fault?' I wondered. I didn't have the energy to get off the floor, so I laid there for hours, thinking.

My head hurt and my lips were sore from the beating they took, but the pain was of no concern to me. All I could think about was what happened. He used me. 'Maybe he didn't love me,' I thought, and that's when the flood hit me, 'Maybe I loved him too much. Maybe I loved him more than he loved me. Maybe we weren't meant to be. Our relationship could never last. He didn't know how to love. He needed too much help. Why did I go down on him? What was I thinking? Of course he wasn't ready for that. It was my fault. I pushed him too hard and then I tried to have sex with him just to stop him from having sex with somebody else. I deserved what I got. I was lucky he didn't try to kill me. That proved that he loved me. Yeah. He loved me. He had to.'

I thought about him a little longer before I decided to peel myself off the floor. I walked to my bed and got in it, hoping that the covers would hide me from reality. I fell asleep and I dreamed that it was all a nightmare and I would wake up in Lionel's arms. The dream felt so real that I woke up looking for Lionel and almost cried when I didn't see him and knew everything had actually happened. Dragging myself out of bed was the hardest part of that day. I called Michael.

"Hello." The sound of his voice made me think everything would be okay. He always made things better.

"He left me, Michael. It's over."

He sighed. "Not this drama again. How about you ask me how my Christmas was and then tell me about the new disaster."

"Sorry. How was your Christmas?"

"Bloody awful," he replied in a British accent. I chuckled involuntarily. "Happy to hear you still have a sense of humor. Now tell me what happened."

"I found out something about him that I shouldn't have, and I confronted him with it. He left last night, but he came back in the wee hours of the morning telling me he was going to have sex with some girl, and then he packed a bag and left again. I don't think he's coming back."

"Well what did you find out?"

"I can't tell you."

"Why not?"

"It's too awful to say out loud."

"Again?"

"No, nothing like the last time, this time it really is too awful to say. It makes me sick just thinking about it."

"Well how can I help?"

"I don't know. Tell me he'll come back, and we'll work this out. Tell me it will be okay."

"I can't do that."

"Why not?"

"Because maybe you two shouldn't be together. All he does is hurt you, and all you do is take it."

"That's not true."

"Yes it is. Maybe this is the best thing that could have happened."

"How can you say that? You know how much I love him."

"And I also know that sometimes love isn't enough."

"But I need to help him. I have to save him."

"Save him from what? Himself! We both know he's his biggest enemy." I sighed. "Leave him alone. If it's meant to be, then he'll find his way back to you and if not then you can be free to find someone who is able to carry on a healthy relationship."

"What? Someone like you?"

"That's not what I meant."

"Yes it is. You're jealous!"

"Right, because I've never had a chance to make a move on you. This is the first time Lionel has fucked up. You're so right! Why just be a friend to you, when we can go back to fucking each other and you can go back to pretending that I'm Lionel. Wow! That's a great idea, just what I wanted for Christmas!"

"Fuck you!" I shouted in to the phone.

"Wouldn't you like to!" he retorted.

I slammed the phone down and paced around the room. I called Michael so he could comfort me and tell me everything would be okay, but instead, he told me it was for the best. He didn't understand that I couldn't give up on Lionel. I knew what had him fucked up in the head and I was determined to help him. I got tired of pacing and decided to take a shower. I got my stuff, put on my robe, and headed to the bathroom. I showered in freezing cold water, trying to torture myself and get my skin to feel as cold as Lionel had treated me. I finally tired of shaking so I got out the shower and put on my robe.

I was slipping on my clothes when I heard a knock at the door. Something inside me thought it was Lionel. I ran to the door and opened it only to find Michael standing there. "How the hell did you get in here?" I asked him as I turned and walked to my dresser to get some socks.

"Some kid signed me in. I told him I wanted to surprise my brother. But none of that is relevant." He shut the door and locked it. I had my back turned to him, but I felt him getting closer. Within a few seconds, his arms were slipping around my waist. I tensed as he pulled me to him. "Tell me what happened," he whispered in my ear. I relaxed a little, but I didn't respond. "I'm here now. It's okay," he assured me.

I didn't want to fall apart again, but I couldn't stop myself. My body trembled as the tears began to fall. "I saw something bad when I went to see Lionel at his home. I saw something real bad. No one should have to live like that. I just want to help him, but he won't let me. He said he hates me." I turned around and buried my face in Michael's neck.

Michael's hands began moving over my back. "It's okay. It's going to be okay."

"It will never be okay."

"Yes it will. It always is. Now let it out."

He didn't have to tell me to let it out, I had already lost control. He started moving towards my bed and he collapsed on it, bringing me down on top of him. I kept crying. As the tears dried up, I thought of how pathetic I was, crying like a baby. I wiped my face on his shirt. "I'm sorry."

"Don't be," he said.

I couldn't face him, so I didn't look at him. "I'm so pathetic," I told him.

"No, you're not."

"Yes, I am."

"No, you're just hurting, and that's okay. We all hurt sometimes."

"Stop saying things like that," I told him as I released a little smile, before I immediately took it back.

"It's true. I've been where you are and it hurts. It hurts like hell, but it's okay. It's supposed to hurt. I'd wonder if you were human if it didn't hurt." He laughed, but I was unable to laugh with him. "Did you eat yet?" he asked.

"No, I'm not hungry."

"You have to eat something. How are you going to be ready for your game tonight if you haven't eaten since" he paused "when was the last time you ate?"

"Yesterday when the bus stopped for lunch."

"You haven't eaten since then?"

"I can't eat."

"Don't be dumb, yes you can. You don't want to, but you can, and you will." He started scooting from under me and he stood up then grabbed my arm, "Now get up." He pulled my arm when I didn't move, so I slowly started to stand. "What happened to your lips?" he asked.

"Nothing."

"Your lips have lots of little cuts."

"Oh." I knew what the cuts were really from, but he didn't need to know. I slipped on some flip-flops and off we went. He took me to a place that served breakfast all day long and then he ordered me a huge breakfast. I told him I didn't want anything, but he didn't listen. After I wolfed down the breakfast, I had to smile.

"Not hungry, huh?" Michael teased.

"I didn't know I was hungry." I laughed and he laughed with me. It felt good to laugh and for a second, my head was filled with something else besides thoughts of Lionel. Michael was a good friend. I was lucky to have him. He wouldn't let my stupidity stop him from being there when I needed him. That's how you know you have a true friend. You curse them out one second and a few seconds later, they're right there to comfort you. In that moment, I appreciated Michael for who he was and how good he had been to me. I was always taking, and he was always giving. I leaned on him harder than I should have, but he didn't care. He smiled at me and I smiled back. At least we were okay.

My smile faded when thoughts of Lionel returned.

Chapter 16

Drowning

"Lionel is an asshole!"

"You're just figuring that out?"

"Michael, don't make it a joke. I mean it! He's an asshole!"

"Calm down."

"How can I calm down? Did you see how he embarrassed me at the game? He made me look like an idiot! I hate him!" Michael raised an eyebrow. "Okay, I don't hate him," I admitted. "I wish I could hate him, but I can't. I love him too much. Uhhhhh! I'm so sick of him!" I threw my jersey across the room. I usually changed in the locker room after games, but I couldn't face my teammates. Because of Lionel, I made a complete ass of myself on the court. He hit me in the back with the ball once and he kept passing the ball either too low or too high for me to get it. The Coach yelled at me a few times and told me to get my head in the game, because it was obviously my fault; the perfect Lionel couldn't be fucking up like that. It was all me. I wasn't listening to him. I wasn't keeping my eyes on the ball. I don't know, maybe some of it really was my fault. I couldn't focus properly. I kept thinking about him and her, and him and Rachel. I usually played about half the game, sharing my minutes with the starting point guard, but because of my messed up playing, and

Lionel's intentional mistakes, I ended up on the bench for the entire second half.

"Wake up."

"Oh, sorry, I got lost in my head for a second."

"Really? I thought you had nothing but space up there." He laughed and I glared at him. "Sorry, now's not the time for jokes."

"Ya think?"

He didn't respond. He sat there and looked off in to thin air. "Are you going to finish changing?" he finally asked.

"Yeah." I kicked off my shoes and removed my shorts. I didn't feel like putting on clothes. I wanted to crawl in my bed and disappear under my sheets.

"It's okay if you don't feel like going anywhere."

"Huh?"

"You're staring at your bed."

"No, I'm just thinking." I paused. "We should get going." I found some clothes and put them on. "Where should we go?"

"We don't have to go anywhere. I know you had a rough day."

"No, I need to go. I can't be in this room. He's everywhere."

"You make it sound like he's haunting you."

"He might as well be."

"You are too much! It hasn't even been a full day since your little spat"

I interrupted, "Can we not talk about it?"

"Sure." He watched as I grabbed my keys. "So where to?"

"I asked you first."

"I know, but I have no idea what you want to do. What do you feel like doing anyway?"

"Getting plastered."

"That won't solve anything. You'll still be sad tomorrow."

"Yeah, but I'll be happy tonight. Now stop being the voice of reason, and let's get out of here." I walked to the door, but he stood still. "Please, Michael, come on."

"Okay, but you decide where we go, and for the record, I think this is the absolute worst thing you could do. There I said it, now let's go."

"Thanks," I told him, making sure he heard the sarcasm in my voice.

I picked a pub down the street, so we weren't outside too long. We walked inside and I was relieved that no one from the basketball team was there. They were probably out celebrating their victory. Michael and I sat down at the bar and my fun began. I lost count after my seventh drink and soon I had a nice buzz going. I remember putting my hand on Michael's thigh and rubbing it, and then him moving my hand.

"We're not going to play that game," he told me. I tried to focus and figure out which one of his heads had said it. He noticed the way I was looking at him. "Okay, I think you've had more than enough. You're going to be sick in the morning."

"I feel great," I said, but I must have been speaking gibberish because both of his heads gave me a funny look. I squinted to get a better look at him.

"I can't believe I let you do this to yourself."

"You're drunk too."

He stared at me for a few seconds. "I'm not drunk."

I wanted to say, 'Oh so you do understand me?' but my brain lost track of the words and I ended up motioning for his beer which resulted in me knocking the beer off the bar and in to his lap. "I'm so sorry," I said or thought. I wasn't sure which.

He stood up and started wiping his pants and I started wiping them too. He grabbed my hand. "I think I got it," he said.

I heard that loud and clear. The bartender gave us our total and I took out some cash, but it didn't look like much. 'Shit!' I thought.

"We have a tab. Remember?" Michael whispered in my ear. His hot breath tickled my skin and I put my arm around his waist in an attempt to pull him closer, but he pulled away. He grabbed my money and put it in my pocket for me then he signed a receipt and got his card back from the bartender. "Let's get you home," he said as he put my arm around him and helped me stand up. My coordination had flown out the window, so he struggled with keeping me on my feet, but somehow he managed.

When we got back to my dorm, I must have signed him in, but I don't remember doing it. I blinked and when I opened my eyes, Michael was undressing me and putting me in bed. He tucked me in like I was a child and then he planted the sweetest, most tender kiss on my forehead. He turned away from me. I reached to grab his arm, but ended up with air. "Don't leave," I said.

"I'm not leaving. I'm sleeping on the floor."

"Hold me."

"I don't think that's a good idea."

"Why not?" I closed my eyes and I could picture him opening his mouth to say something. "I'm drunk. Don't argue. Hold me." I forced my eyes open. I was searching for his face, but I settled for the ceiling instead. "Please." The light from the room seemed to burn my eyes so I closed them again. I fell asleep. As I began to stir, I felt someone snuggled up behind me. My initial thought was Lionel, but then I remembered that I had been with Michael. I was still feeling the effects of the alcohol, but that's no excuse for what I did next. I started contracting my ass and soon his dick was coming to life. I tried to think of the last time Michael had fucked me, but my brain couldn't focus on more than one thing at a time and I desperately wanted to feel someone inside me.

After a few minutes, he whispered, "What do you think you're doing?"

"Fuck me," I whispered back.

Apparently it was too low for him to hear. "What did you say?"

"Fuck me." I started really grinding my ass in to him.

"I can't." He moved the arm that was draped around me and started to get up.

"If you don't, I'll find someone else who will." A thought hit me. "Is Henry in?"

"Shut up. You can't even get out the bed without my help." I felt him get up. I turned on my back and I looked at him.

"I can move fine." I sat up on the side of the bed then I moved to get up, but the dizziness was too much. I almost fell but he caught me. If I was sober, I would have realized that I couldn't have planned it better myself.

"Take me," I whispered in his ear as he lowered me on to the bed.

"You're drunk."

"So."

"I don't want you like this."

"You're drunk, too."

"No, I think you sobered me up already." He surprised me with a warm smile.

"So what's the problem?" I asked as I found his face with my hand and rubbed his cheek. The distance between us grew as he stood up again.

"You're the problem."

"Oh, no problems here. None." I rubbed my hardon through my boxers.

"You love Lionel."

"And what does that have to do with us?"

"It has everything to do with us. I don't want just part of you."

"You never cared before. Why can't you just fuck me like you use to? You were good at it." I knew I was whining but I didn't care.

"Wow, lucid enough to string a few sentences together," he said with his voice laced in sarcasm.

"Don't use big words."

"Like what?"

"Lucid."

"It has five letters," he told me.

"So does fuck me."

He laughed. "Um, no, try again."

"Please?"

"Nope, still not there yet."

Blame the alcohol, but his smug demeanor pissed me off. "What is your deal? You act as if you've never put your dick in me before, like you're scared or something."

"Don't you get it?"

"What?"

"Oh God! You are dense!" He stared at me. "Uhh! I guess I can tell you. You're too drunk to remember this in the morning."

"Yes I will."

"Sure." He crawled in bed next to me.

"What are you doing?"

"Ssh." I quickly locked away my anger and turned to my side so he could spoon me. My eyes were starting to close again. "I know Lionel hurts you more than what you tell me about." That's the last line I remember him saying, but he gave me a whole speech. "I'm fairly certain that the cuts on your lips are somehow his fault, but I know you'll never admit it. Sometimes I fear he might kill you and that scares me because you're my buddy and I love you. Not sexual, well a little sexual, but I know you belong to Lionel and I'm not desperate enough to settle for half your heart. Besides, you're not really my type anymore. You've let him change everything about you. I look at you sometimes and I wonder where my Lucas went. I'll always be your friend, but I don't know how much longer I can sit around and watch you destroying your life over a stupid high school dream guy who has turned your life in to a nightmare. Don't you miss the old you? The one who didn't cry all the time? The one who didn't need Lionel to make him feel whole? The one who was strong enough and man enough to stand on his own two feet? I've been looking for him for a while now. I hope I find him soon." I was snoring by that point. He kissed my neck and then whispered, "I know Lucas is still in there somewhere. Come back Lucas. Come back."

I woke up and almost had a heart attack when I opened my eyes and saw Lionel standing over us. "Lionel?"

"You couldn't even wait a day!" He shouted. "I knew you would shack up with Michael as soon as I left, but even I didn't think you would do this shit this soon!"

The shouting woke Michael. "What's going" he opened his eyes before he finished his question then he jumped away from me. "It's not what it looks like," he told Lionel.

"I know. You both accidentally fell out of your clothes."

"Nothing happened! We still have on boxers you idiot!" Michael threw off the covers. Michael stood up and got in Lionel's face. "You know you have some nerve coming in here trying to be the jealous boyfriend! Especially after that stunt you pulled yesterday."

"He told you?" I never saw a black person look pale before, but that's the best word to describe Lionel's face. He looked sick and I was waiting for him to hurl right there.

"Yes, I know all about how you walked out on him so you could go fuck some girl."

"Oh, that. I"

"What do you mean, 'Oh that.' What did you think I was talking about?"

"Lucas you better get your friend out of my face before I hurt him," Lionel said.

Michael turned and looked at me as I struggled to sit up on the bed. I was experiencing the mother of all hangovers. I felt like

I had blacked out the night before because I only remembered bits and pieces. I wasn't even sure we hadn't done anything, but I knew if Mike said it, then it must be the truth. I startled myself when my lips parted and out came, "Maybe you should leave Michael."

"What about you? I don't want to leave you alone with him when he's like this."

"Like what?" Lionel asked as he stepped closer to Michael.

"Like a crazy person."

Michael shouldn't have said that. Lionel grabbed him and forced him to the door. He opened the door and forced Michael out then he grabbed some clothes and a pair of shoes and threw them at Michael. "Don't come back!" he warned. He closed the door and turned to look at me.

I knew it was the alcohol, but I didn't really care much either way whether Michael was there or not. All I knew was Lionel was home. "You gave him my pants," I stated.

"Why did you have him over here?" Lionel asked.

"Why did you fuck that girl?" As I was asking the question, I started feeling really sick and all I could think about was putting my head back on the pillow. I didn't give him time to answer. "Don't answer that. Look, I have a hangover. Let's just do this later." I stretched out on the bed and pulled the covers up before I put my head on the pillow and closed my eyes. Hangovers trumped arguments any day.

Suddenly the covers were ripped off of me and hands were on my arm, pulling me off the bed. I hit the floor with a loud thud, succeeding in knocking the wind out of my lungs. Thankfully, my ass cushioned the fall and I only lightly bumped my head. "No, we're going to talk now!"

I took a minute to catch my breath. "Would you stop doing shit like that?" It was more of a thought, but I said the words out loud. He flipped me over and pulled down my boxers. My voice cracked as I asked, "What are you doing?" I didn't feel queasy from the hangover because the adrenaline was rushing through my veins and all I could think about was what Lionel was going to do to me.

"Checking to see if you let him fuck you."

I reached down and pulled my boxers up. "My ass does not belong to you. You made that clear yesterday." There was a long silence that drained my adrenaline and returned the queasiness. I started to feel lethargic and that's when I wondered what he was doing. "Lionel?"

He smacked me hard on my ass and it stung. "Don't you ever talk to me like that again!"

"Or what?" I asked him as a yawn escaped my lips. I expected him to hit me, but instead, the silence returned. I whispered, "I can't believe I'm so tired." I was almost in dream land again.

Then came the knock at the door. "Security. Open up!" I knew it was Michael's doing, and so did Lionel. "I'm going to kill Michael!" he shouted as he walked to the door. I closed my eyes and fell asleep again.

Chapter 17

The Buzzkill

There were voices all around me. It sounded like people were arguing about something. I thought I heard someone say my name then I felt someone lift my head off the floor.

"Lucas!" They shook me. "Wake up Lucas!"

My eyelids felt like sandbags as I tried to force them open. There was a hint of light and it stung my eyes so I squeezed them shut.

"Lucas! Dammit! Stop playing games and open your eyes!"

I knew that voice; that was Lionel. I wanted to see him. I willed my eyes open and soon I was looking in someone's face, but it wasn't Lionel. The face was familiar though. Michael. Yeah, that's who it was. It was Michael. I smiled at him. "Hi, Mike," I said.

"Are you okay?" he asked.

"Um." Hands came out of nowhere and started pulling me to my feet.

"He's fine! Now go away."

"Why don't you let him tell us that Lionel?"

My body was pressed against someone. I leaned further in to them, trying to balance myself and stop the room from spinning.

I put my head on the person's shoulder and smelled them. They smelled like Lionel.

"Lucas. Are you okay, Lucas?" I turned my head to the side and saw Henry.

"Henry?" I asked.

"What did he do to you?"

"Nothing. I'm drunk, but Lionel's here now, so I'm okay."

"See, everything is fine. Now get the hell out of our room!" I felt Lionel's chest vibrate as he spoke. I put my arms around him and pulled him closer, not caring who was watching.

"Lionel, just shut up," Michael said.

"Is there a problem here or not?" asked a voice I didn't recognize.

"I keep telling you everything is fine. He fell out of bed, that's all."

I felt a hand on my shoulder. "Is that true?"

I turned and looked at the person. The security guard was shorter than me. He had black hair on the sides of his head with a bald spot on the top. "Yes, I fell. I'm fine." I put my head back against Lionel's shoulder and took a deep breath. I wanted everyone to go away and leave us alone. "Everyone can leave now. I'm okay."

"What the hell is wrong with you?" Michael shouted. "I heard him yelling at you! Tell us what he did! I know he did something!"

"Why don't you shut the fuck up and leave! Nobody wants you here." Lionel told him.

Michael grabbed me and pulled me away from Lionel. He turned me around so I could face him. "Look at me!" I focused on him. "He hurt you and we both know it, but you can do whatever the hell you want to do. Just don't keep pulling me in to this shit!" He shook me. "You need to snap out of it!"

I wasn't able to warn him before my mouth opened and the alcohol in my stomach came spewing out, landing all over his shirt and pants. Lionel came up behind me and grabbed me to keep me from falling. He held me gently then rubbed my back and helped me over to my bed. He sat me down and grabbed a t-shirt off the floor and wiped my mouth and whispered, "Are you okay?"

His gentleness and genuine tone of concern was surprising. I caught myself thinking, 'He does care.'

"Do you need a trashcan? Are you going to be sick again?" His eyes seemed to smile at me.

"I feel a little better." I looked at Michael. "I'm sorry."

"It's okay, these are your pants anyway." He walked over to a pile of clothes on the floor and grabbed his pants. We all watched him as he turned his back to us and changed pants then he took off his shirt and picked up one of my shirts. "I'm just borrowing this," he said as he pulled my shirt over his head.

"Okay."

"Where did the security guard go?" Michael asked when he turned around.

"He left," Henry said. "Maybe we should leave too. I don't think we're going to get anywhere by staying."

"I don't think so either, but at least we tried," Michael responded. Both of them seemed to be ignoring us.

"Good, now leave," Lionel told them.

They both walked towards the door. Michael stopped at the doorway and looked at me. Our eyes locked and I knew he would be there if I needed him. "Goodbye Lucas," he said in a voice barely above a whisper.

I shook my head and Michael and Henry left, closing the door behind them. Lionel walked over and locked the door. He picked up the vomit covered clothes and put them in his dirty clothes bag before he came back to the bed and gingerly rubbed my cheek. "Just get some sleep and we'll talk later." I lied back in the bed and he pulled the covers up over me. "Do you need anything?"

I wanted to ask Lionel what had gotten in to him but I liked the change too much to say anything and risk the return of the old him. "No thank you."

"Okay. You get some rest." I turned to my side and tried to relax, but my stomach still felt weird.

"Lionel?"

"Yes," his voice sounded far away. I turned around to find him, but I didn't see him anywhere. "Yes?" he said again. This time his head appeared at the side of my bed.

"Hi," I said, startled by his location. "What are you doing?"

"I was doing a few push-ups."

"Oh." I paused for a second to allow my brain to understand what he was doing. "I think I need some water."

"Okay." He got up off the floor and went to our fridge. He took out a bottle of water and brought it to me. I watched him open it. "Here." I sat up and he was at my side trying to soothe me.

After a few sips of water, I didn't want anymore. "Thanks," I told him. He put the bottle on the desk next to my bed. He moved back to the floor. "How long are you going to be down there?"

"I don't know."

"Well why don't you take a break?"

"And do what?"

"Hold me?" I needed to feel someone's arms around me, making me feel safe.

He stopped moving and was perfectly still for a few seconds. "Okay," he whispered.

I turned around so he could spoon with me and I listened as he took off his clothes. I let out a gasp when I felt his hard dick against my boxer covered ass. "Lionel that's not what I meant."

"Sorry. It won't go down."

"Well put your boxers back on."

"I'll behave." I felt his dick jump.

"What got you so excited anyway?"

"This guy asked me to hold him and all I could think about was his ass grinding on my dick." He held me for a few minutes and his nose brushed against the back of my neck. "I did this to you, didn't I?

"Did what?" I became aware that I was pushing against him.

"The drinking. You went out and got fucked up because of me." I didn't say anything. "You don't have to answer. I know it's my fault." Again, I was silent. I wasn't tired anymore; I just wasn't in the mood to have a conversation. "I made up Rachel. There was no girl waiting to have sex with me, I only wanted to hurt you." He kissed my neck. "I hate knowing that you know me. I fucking freaked, and I'm sorry, but I couldn't talk about it then. I still don't want to talk about it." He leaned close to my ear. "Why do you want me to remember? I try so hard to fucking forget it, and you want me to remember?" His hand landed on my hip. "Do you want me to tell you about it?"

I wanted to say, 'no' but I feared he would never be willing to open up again. "Okay."

His hand came around to the front of my boxers and slipped inside. He grabbed my soft dick and started stroking it. I wanted to tell him to stop, but I didn't. "I don't know what happened while I was there," he said, "all I know is I woke up and she was next to me, naked. Is that what you want to hear?" I kept quiet. "Or how about how my father used to beat me when I was a kid? How about that? Do you want to know how many times he whooped my ass just because I was there? Or how about how the whole fucking family knew, but nobody stopped him from hurting me?" His grip tightened on my dick. "Oh, no, I know what you want to hear! You want me to tell you about the first time she did me. I was twelve. I was big for my age, in more ways than one." He started grinding his dick against me. "That bitch got me drunk and took advantage of me. That's what you want to hear, right? She asked if I wanted to learn about sex, and I told her yes. My father found out a few months later." His voice sounded shaky. "I really wanted to go to this birthday party and she told me I had to fuck her to get permission. Stupid kid that I was, I did it. My father caught us and it was hell to pay. You would think he would go after her, maybe even kill her, but not him. He beat me so bad that I was in the hospital for a week. When I came out, he was gone and it was just me and her. She blamed me for chasing him off, so she was extra rough on me. How about that? Is that good?"

I realized he was off in a world of his own and he didn't expect an answer from me. He continued, "I was as tall as her, and no doubt stronger, but I would never hurt her so I took whatever she dished out. It was our little secret, but I knew it was a dirty secret and I didn't want it. I complained so much about it that when I was fourteen, she sold me to two guys for a weekend. We needed the money and I needed to be taught a fucking lesson. Pun intended. Those guys fucked me all weekend and I came back appreciating her more. At least I got to get off when I did her. Is this the type of shit you want to hear?" He licked my ear as his hand sped up on my dick. I was still soft, but he didn't care. "Well I got more. I cut her off when I went to play basketball over the summer. She was okay with it because she had a boyfriend." He nibbled on my ear for a second before he blew hot air over it, causing a strange sensation of warm where his tongue hadn't been, and cool, where his saliva was still drying. "I didn't know they broke up until I went home. Ronnie was there so everything was normal until the day before we left. I had a few drinks and she must have spiked my beer because the next thing I knew, I was waking up next to her. Is that enough for you, or do you want to hear some more, because I've got more."

His hand gave up on trying to get me off, and he moved his hand to rest on my stomach as he held me in place while he ground against me.

"That's enough," I told him.

His pace quickened. He was moaning. 'Stop!' I thought, but again, I remained silent. I stayed still. I felt something dropping on my neck. His moans never stopped. Finally, his cum erupted and landed on the outside of my boxers.

"I'm sorry," he told me as his hand glided up and down my chest.

'He's crying! Oh my God, he's crying,' I thought, as I realized what was dripping on my neck. "It's okay," I said.

"No, it's not." I felt him pull away from me.

He got up and I heard him putting his clothes on. What was I supposed to say to him? What was I supposed to feel? I had too many thoughts running around in my head and I couldn't grab hold of any of them. That's when I saw the little boy's face as he opened the door that day. "How old is Ronnie," I wondered out loud.

"What?"

I couldn't believe he heard me. "How old is Ronnie?" I turned around to see his face.

"Six. I showed a girl down the street what I had been taught and seven and a half months later, she was popping out a preemie. She kept him until she got her new boyfriend, then her parents kept him, but they died in a car accident over the summer so they gave him to me, even though I guess technically I don't have him."

I wondered why there wasn't a hint of emotion. "How come I never saw him before?"

"She takes care of him, not me."

"Is it okay to leave him with her?"

"She won't hurt him."

"But"

"Just shut up!" I looked at him and his wall was back in place. "Don't look at me like that!" He sounded like his old self again.

"Like what?"

"Like there's something wrong with me. I'm not broken! I don't need you to fix me because I'm doing fine on my own."

"Right and what you just told me was perfectly normal," I said under my breath.

He swung and hit me upside my head. "Shut up!"

'Maybe Michael was right. Maybe Lionel was crazy,' I thought as I grabbed my head.

"I'm sorry. I didn't mean to hit you."

"You never do." He backhanded me. "I suppose your hand slipped," I told him sarcastically. Something was wrong with me. I couldn't shut up. His hands went around my neck and he squeezed, blocking my next sentence in my throat.

"Would you shut the fuck up?" he screamed as his fingers pressed in to my neck. I brought my hands up and scratched his arms, but there was nothing I could do to make him stop. The room started to go black and I wondered if my eyelids were closing or if I was dying.

Chapter 18

Free Falling

I opened my eyes and immediately grabbed my neck. My throat hurt like hell and I wasn't sure why. "Thank God you're alive," whispered a voice behind me. Then the person gently kissed my neck.

"Lionel?" A sharp pain shot through my throat as I spoke. My voice came out hoarse.

"It's okay. I'm here."

"What happened?"

"You don't remember?"

"No." He squeezed me tighter and kissed my neck again. I felt his limp dick press against my boxers which pressed against my skin. I had a flash of me with boxers on and him cumming on me. Then my mind flipped through images of Lionel hitting me and choking me. I jumped away from him. "Please don't touch me," I whispered as I turned to face him and I moved as far away as I could until my back hit the wall.

He moved close to me. "I'm sorry. I didn't mean to hurt you." I couldn't look at him, but I couldn't force myself to turn away either. "You know I love you." He reached out and tried to place a hand on my leg, but I moved my leg away. "Don't be like that. I said I was sorry."

"Get away from me." I kicked at him, trying to get him out of the bed. He grabbed my left foot and I kicked him in the chest with my right. He let go of my foot and I kicked him repeatedly until I had successfully kicked him off the bed.

"Calm down!" he shouted.

"You tried to kill me," I croaked, barely above a whisper.

"I would never try to kill you. I just lost it for a second, but I never wanted to hurt you."

"That's the problem. You never want to hurt me, but it seems like that's the only thing you're good at."

"Don't say that shit!"

"It's the truth." I had to cough to clear my throat. "I know you don't want to hurt me. I know you can't help yourself and that's what scares me. What's going to happen the next time you lose it?"

"It won't happen again. I promise."

"You can't promise that and I'm not going to ask you to." I slowly started to stand. "We can't live together anymore."

"What?" he asked.

"You heard me. We can't live together anymore."

"Where do you expect me to go?"

"Nowhere. I'm going to leave."

"But you can't."

"I have to." I reached under my bed and grabbed my duffle bag.

"You can't be serious," he said as I walked over to my dresser and started packing clothes. He walked up behind me and pulled me close to him. "Don't leave me," he begged. I kept packing. I felt his hand rub down my stomach before slipping inside my boxers and landing on my soft dick.

"Stop." His tongue glided along my neck. I pushed him off of me. "I said stop." He looked stunned. I found some clothes and put them on and then I continued packing.

"How can you do this?" he asked when I zipped my bag.

"How can I not?" I picked up my bag and grabbed my wallet. "I'll be back for the rest of my things." He blocked the door. I took a quick second to glance over his beautiful body. Allowing my eyes to take in his chocolate skin and luscious lips before tracing a path down his chiseled abs. I found myself licking my lips as I looked at the monster between his legs and then I looked back at his face, reminding myself that I had to give all of it up. I had to give him up.

"What do I have to do?"

"Get out of my way and let me leave."

"I can't do that."

"It's the only thing I'm asking you to do. This is already hard enough so please just get out of the way."

"Ask me to do something else. I'll do anything." I tried to walk by him, but he pulled me in to a hug. "Damn! Come on Lucas, don't do this shit to me. What do you want me to do?" he hissed in my ear. He dropped down on his knees, keeping his arms around me and almost breaking me in two with the death grip he had on my waist. "I'm begging you. Don't leave me. I'll get help. Just tell me what you want me to do. Please?"

I looked down at Lionel's head pressed in to my stomach and said simply, "Let me go." I tried to pull one of his arms off of me.

"No, I'm not letting you go again. Neither of us is leaving this room until we get some shit straight!"

"I can't stay here."

"Yes you can and you will. I know if you leave this time you might never come back and I'm not going to take that risk. You're staying."

His grip loosened a little and I broke free. "I'm sorry." I opened the door and he quickly kicked it shut with his foot.

"I don't know what I'll do if you leave me," he said in a less frantic tone. Something about the way he said it stopped me from reaching for the door again.

We all have those moments in our lives where our mind tells us the right thing to do, but our heart overpowers all reason. I should have opened the door and walked away from him; instead, I allowed him to pull me back in. "You're not going to hurt yourself, are you?"

"I don't know. I mean my life is fucked up. I'm fucked up. Everything is fucked up. It's not like anyone would miss me anyway. I'm just another screwed up black kid."

"Lionel don't talk like that."

"Why not? It's true. You don't even want to love me anymore. You're leaving me." He paused before saying, "Everyone leaves me."

I dropped my bag, defeated. "I'm not leaving you. Okay, are you okay now? I'm not going anywhere."

"Maybe you should leave me. I don't deserve you. You're too good of a person to be stuck with someone like me. I can't be normal like you, no matter how hard I try."

"I'm not normal," I said as I sat down on the floor next to him.

"Yes you are and I've ruined us." He sat back on his feet. "I hate myself. I knew I shouldn't have fucked around with you. I tried to leave you alone, but it was too hard and now I'm losing you."

I grabbed his face and turned it to me. "You're not losing me, at least not tonight." I stared deep in to his eyes and then I leaned forward and kissed him. "See, I'm still here."

His response was to pull me in to a longer kiss. I spent the first second of the kiss thinking about how horrible my breath was. Then I was distracted by my mind yelling at me for being dumb enough to stay. He stopped kissing me and said, "I'm going to get help. Just promise you won't leave me."

"I promise."

He put his hand on my shorts. "Let me make you happy like I used to."

I pushed his hand away. It was his nature to turn to sex to solve our situation, but I didn't want to. "That's our first problem. Sex can't fix what's wrong with us."

"Maybe not, but I know it'll make you feel better."

I stood up to get away from him. "I'm staying, but we're not sleeping in the same bed. I'll sleep in mine and you sleep in yours."

"But I sleep better when I have you in my arms. At least let me hold you until I fall asleep."

"I can't." He looked as if I had punched him in the face. "Look, it's not because I don't want to. I do. It's bad enough I'm staying here with you! We both know what we're like in bed together and I don't trust you to behave. Hell I don't trust myself in bed with you."

He looked at me with sorrow in his eyes. "Fine. As long as you stay." I took off my shoes and got in my bed, fully dressed. He sat for a few minutes after I moved and then he finally peeled himself off the floor and got in his bed. "Lucas," he called.

"Yes."

"Thanks for staying."

"You're welcome." He was quiet after that besides the sounds of him tossing and turning in his bed. I listened to him for hours before I dozed off. I woke up the next afternoon with a familiar feeling of warmth around me and I involuntarily smiled when I realized Lionel had crawled in bed with me and he was holding me. My smile got even wider when I turned around and saw he was wearing boxers.

I reached out and tapped him lightly. His eyes opened slowly. "I'm sorry. I couldn't sleep," he said almost immediately. I wondered what he did for sleep all those years before we slept together and that's when thoughts of her entered my head again. My face fell and Lionel started pulling away from me. "I didn't mean to upset you."

"It's fine. It's not you. I just thought about something."

"About what?"

"Let's not talk about it, right now." I leaned in and kissed him. "I'm going to go get cleaned up." I rolled over him and got out of bed.

"Can I come with you?" he asked.

"The answer to that question has always been no, and today is no different." I looked down at him and stroked his cheek. "Nice try, though." I gathered my stuff and went to take my shower. The shower took forever because I kept zoning out on random thoughts. I thought about how odd it felt to be so intimate with him. I thought about my decision to stay. I thought about possibly making the biggest mistake of my life. I thought about losing him forever. That thought scared the shit out of me. I spent so many years of my life wanting him and he was finally mine. Sure he was damaged more than most, but he was still mine. If I couldn't fix him, who could?

I felt a draft and I looked over to see Lionel peeping through my curtain, leering at me. "How long are you going to be in there?"

"I'm almost done. Why? Have I been in here a long time?"

"Long enough for me to take a shower and get dressed. For a second, I thought you ran away." He let out a nervous laugh.

"I told you I wasn't leaving and I meant it. You don't have to worry about that."

"I guess I'll see you when you get out then," he said with a smile on his face.

"Okay." He closed the curtain and I tried to quickly finish my shower. I stepped out of the shower and wrapped a towel around my waist. As I stood in front of the sink taking out my toothbrush and toothpaste, Henry walked in.

"Hey," he said.

"Hey." I glanced at my reflection in the mirror and I was ashamed of my bruises so I looked down at the sink.

"Look, it's none of my business, but"

"You're right, it's not," I told him, trying to stop him before he gave me his opinion.

"My uncle used to beat on my aunt," he said. "She would show up at our house late at night with bruises all over. Sometimes she had broken bones. I remember one time he broke her finger because she didn't turn off the light fast enough. My mother begged her to leave him, but she used to tell my mother that she was just jealous because she didn't have a man. Things went on that way for a long time until three years ago. It was the middle of the night when my twelve year-old cousin showed up at the door with his little brother and sister. My mother asked them where their mother was and the little one said, 'Dad said Mommy's with God now.' I had to catch my mother because her knees gave out. A few minutes later, she was calling the police and sending them to her sister's house." He stopped to wipe his right eye. "Of course it was too late when they got there. We found out later that he left her on the floor, bleeding to death. It took her hours to die." He wiped his eye again. "Can you imagine what she must have gone through? Oh, and let's not even talk about the trauma to her children and my mother. It's been three years and I don't think any of them are over it yet." A hesitant laugh escaped from his lips. "I mean look at me. I'm doing the best out of everyone and thinking about it still brings me close to tears. Every time I go home and see my cousins with my mother, I remember how they got there and it hurts like hell to think that all my aunt had to do was leave him. How can you love anyone more than you love yourself? Or love a man more than your children? I'm not telling you what to do about Lionel, because it's your business, but I will tell you this: don't love him more than you love yourself. If something happens to you, your family and friends aren't going to miss the way you loved

Lionel, they're going to miss you. I want you to think about your family the next time he hits you. Picture the look on your mother's face when she has to come identify your body at the morgue, because that's where your relationship is headed."

"Thanks for the memo," I said in a harsher tone than I intended, "I'll be sure to keep that in mind."

"Did you hear a word I said?"

"I heard everything you said, and I'm sorry about your aunt, but I'm not her and Lionel's not her husband. Lionel is going to get help and everything is going to be better."

"My uncle got help a few times. He was always good for that first month and then it was as if nothing had changed."

"Henry! Will you please back off? I am fine! Okay?"

"Okay." He started walking towards a shower. "I know we're not really friends but please remember that you can come talk to me whenever you need to."

I shook my head and he got in the shower. The bathroom seemed smaller for some reason, like the walls were trying to fall in on me. I finished brushing my teeth and I attempted to look at myself in the mirror. I was surprised when I couldn't look myself in the eye.

When I entered our room, Lionel was doing some sit-ups. He stopped and sat up. "How are you feeling?" he asked.

"Like I was hit by a train," I told him as I forced a smile on my face.

He didn't smile back at me. "I'm sorry," he said.

"Don't keep apologizing."

"I have to."

The rest of the day was awkward. Lionel was tip-toeing around me, constantly apologizing for everything. We went out to dinner after practice but neither of us had much to say, so we ate in silence, throwing in the occasional comment. When night came, Lionel and I cuddled up in my bed and fell asleep.

A few days later, we were still slightly uncomfortable around each other, but things were getting better. He had gone to the school medical center to get information on therapy and anger management classes. He decided he would rather go to therapy than do the classes. He talked to Coach and told him he had personal issues and he wanted to speak with the school therapist. Coach was shocked but he said he was pleased that Lionel was trying to take care of himself both physically and mentally. He made a few phone calls and told Lionel the school would foot the bill, but he had to wait until the new semester started. I was pleased that he wouldn't have to pay for it and that he was going to get the help he needed. Unfortunately, we still had two weeks before his first session was scheduled.

Chapter 19

Rock Bottom

"I can't believe you're still with him, after everything he's done."

"You promised we wouldn't talk about Lionel."

"That was before I saw you. Have you looked in the mirror lately?"

Of course I had. I knew there was a bruise with a long red scratch down the right side of my face from Lionel slapping me with his belt buckle the night before. "Dammit Michael!"

"Fine, we don't have to talk about it. You're not going to listen anyway." He picked up his menu.

"He's going to get help and things are going to be better. You'll see."

"Right, because one therapy session is going to magically cure him, and everything will be okay. Who cares if he accidentally kills you between now and next Tuesday? It's no big deal."

"I wish you would stop saying that. He's not going to kill me!"

"A week and a half ago you said he was never going to hit you again. But I'm sure he didn't mean it, right? It was an accident, just an innocent reflex."

"Michael, you don't understand. I'm not the victim here; he is. I know he has a short fuse and sometimes I do things to provoke him. I can't be surprised when he lashes out at me."

"Oh great, you're still making excuses for him! There is no reason for him to ever put his hands on you," he rolled his eyes, "but whatever." There was a pause while he opened his menu and then he said, "I thought you said you didn't want to talk about him."

"I don't." Michael pretended to study the menu. "Don't be that way Michael."

"What way?"

"You know damn well you're not really looking at the menu. You're going to order the flapjack special and we both know it."

"That doesn't mean I can't look at the options."

He must have read each item on the menu before he looked up at me again. I knew I had to change the subject, "So what are you going to do this afternoon?"

"I don't know. What are you going to do?" I was relieved that he sounded normal.

"I think I'm just going to go back to my room and get some rest. These early morning practices are kicking my ass."

His expression changed when he looked over my shoulder. "What the hell is he doing here?"

I turned around and saw Lionel walking towards us. He came over to my table and sat down next to me. "What are you doing here?" I asked.

"I got bored in the room without you, so I decided to come eat with you guys."

Michael said, "He's only been gone like ten minutes."

"But it was ten minutes too long. You know I can't stand to have him out of my sight." Lionel put his arm around my shoulder and squeezed.

"Lucas, um, why don't we have breakfast together another time?" Michael stared directly at Lionel. "I seem to have lost my appetite."

"Come on Michael, just stay," I told him as he stood up.

"I can't." He grabbed his coat and said, "See you later, Lucas."

I called after him as he walked away, "Michael!" He didn't turn around.

"Don't call him," Lionel barked. His tone made me flinch. In a softer voice, he whispered "Relax, Lucas. Damn, Michael really has you on edge." Lionel sat back in his chair. "What's his problem anyway?"

"I think you know," I told him.

"Oh, he's still pissed off because I kicked him out of our room that night?"

"That must be it," I said.

"He needs to get over that. I told him I was sorry."

"Uh-huh," I whispered.

"So what were you two talking about?"

"Nothing."

"I saw the two of you. You were talking about something and it looked pretty heated for a minute."

"How long were you watching us?"

"I followed you here to make sure you were okay, and then I stayed after I saw the two of you hugging. Why were you hugging him?"

"He's my friend. I hug him all the time."

"Well I don't want you hugging him again." I didn't say anything. "Did you hear me?" he hissed.

"Yes, I heard you."

"Good, now where's the waitress, I'm ready to eat."

The waitress came over and we placed our order. I thought Lionel would move to the other side of the table, but he didn't. We talked about practice and the upcoming game and the new semester and we both carefully avoided certain subjects, such as Michael, the night before and Lionel's upcoming therapy. We were almost done eating when a few guys from the basketball team came up to our table.

"What's up guys?" asked one of them.

"Not much," Lionel said.

"So, um, Lucas, have you always been so accident prone?" Troy asked.

"Huh?"

He laughed. "Lionel told us you're a skater and that's how you get all those strange bruises. You must be really hardcore."

"Ha, guess I am."

"I skate a little. Nothing near your level, but I try. We should get together some time and go to the park."

"Um."

"See Troy, I told you he wouldn't want to go. He never does anything social," said James.

Troy sat down at our table. "What are you doing?" asked Lionel.

"You're cool Lionel, but Lucas here is, um, I don't know. He's different." Troy looked at me. "Why don't you hang out with us?"

"I have a lot of homework."

"That's bull! We all have homework, but we still find time to hang out, even Lionel hangs out sometimes."

"Well"

"Look, I'm not trying to force you to talk to us. I'm just letting you know that we've noticed you don't really interact with us much. You spend all your time in your room or with Lionel." Troy stood. "Give me a call when you get tired of looking at his ugly mug."

"Okay," I said. When the guys left our table, I wasn't sure what had happened. It was true I didn't have much to say to them, and that included during practice and games, but I didn't think it was a big deal. Then I remembered the other thing Troy said. That was hilarious. "You told them I was a skater?" I asked Lionel. He didn't answer. "Lionel?" He still didn't answer. I followed his gaze to the table where Troy was sitting then I tapped Lionel on his shoulder.

"What?"

"Nothing," I said, recognizing his tone immediately.

Five minutes later, we had paid the bill and were walking back to our dorm. Lionel hadn't spoken, so I was worried about what was going on in his head and I went over our morning to figure out what I might have done to upset him.

At the dorm, the elevator was taking a long time to come, so Lionel said, "Let's take the stairs."

"Okay." Lionel opened the door to the stairwell and I saw Henry coming down. He stopped and stared at us. Lionel started walking up the stairs and I felt the need to say something to Henry before we reached him. "Hey, Henry."

"Hey."

"What's wrong with the elevators?" Lionel asked.

"One of the elevators is broken and the other one is stopping on every floor."

"Oh."

Henry grabbed my arm as I walked by him. "What happened to your face?" he asked.

"He had an accident," Lionel said. Then Lionel grabbed my arm and pulled me away from Henry. We were almost to our floor when Lionel started in on me. "I can't believe you!"

"I'm sorry." I didn't know what I had done, but I knew I should apologize.

"How dare you disrespect me like that!"

"What did I do?"

"Let's see, you flirted with Troy,"

"What?"

"Shut up! You flirted with him. You flirted with Michael. You flirted with Henry. Who else have you been flirting with?" He pulled me to him and gripped my arm even tighter.

"I wasn't flirting with them."

"Yes you were!" He let go of my arm and punched me in the gut. I leaned forward and grabbed my stomach. I had hoped we would make it to the room before he started. He grabbed my arm again and pulled me up the last few stairs, "Come on!"

"No!" I yelled as I tried to pull my arm away from him. He responded by squeezing my arm and pulling me to him.

"You really fucked up now!" he shouted as he pushed me away and let go of my arm. I stumbled on the steps and lost my balance. Suddenly everything was in slow motion. He had a look of horror on his face as he reached forward to try to grab me. He was too late. I saw him standing at the top of the stairs and I saw the white ceiling and the light, then everything went black. I opened my eyes and Lionel was kneeling next to me. "I'm sorry," he said. I couldn't feel anything. I closed my eyes and when I opened them again, I saw Henry running towards me.

He pushed Lionel away from me. "Get away from him! I heard you, you sick freak!" They both disappeared.

I heard voices. My eyes fluttered. I tried opening my eyes. "He's waking up," someone said.

I finally succeeded in opening my eyes and I saw Michael and Henry and my mother and father. My mother was by my side immediately. "Do you know who I am?"

I tried to shake my head, but my head hurt too much to move. "Yes," I croaked, but it sounded more like 'ssss' than anything else.

My mother moved back and a doctor was soon standing over me. "Lucas, do you know where you are?"

"Sssss."

"Do you know what happened?"

I pictured Lionel at the top of the stairs. "Sssss."

"What's wrong with him?" asked my mother. "Why can't he talk?"

"He's been out for two weeks. Give him a little time. His tests didn't show any brain damage, but you can never tell when there's been that much swelling." The doctor shined a light in my eyes. "Lucas, are you in a lot of pain?"

"Ess."

He turned to someone in the room. "Set up a morphine drip." Then he turned back to me. "Try to move your fingers." I did. Everyone smiled. "Okay good," he said. He moved the cover off my legs. "Now try to move your toes." That's when I realized I couldn't feel my legs. I tried to move my toes, but there was nothing. He turned his back to me and blocked my foot then he looked at me and asked, "Did you feel anything?"

"No." 'What's wrong?' I thought. "Wa wong?" was what came out.

"The nurse will be back to set up your morphine drip, then you can just press the button whenever you feel pain," he said. "Try to relax and don't worry." The doctor turned to my parents, "May I see the two of you in the hall for a moment?"

I watched them walk out the door. Michael walked next to me and grabbed my hand. His touch felt comforting so I squeezed his hand. "He's squeezing my hand," Michael said to Henry.

"That's a good sign."

I was afraid I was paralyzed. I focused on my words and then I started to ask the question, "Am I,"

"You're fine," Michael said, "You're going to be just fine."

"Lionel?"

"Don't worry about him," Michael whispered as he gently stroked my cheek with his finger, tracing an imaginary line.

"I'm sure he's getting what he deserves," Henry said.

Chapter 20

Beginning the Comeback

My mother called the police and told them I was up. Michael and Henry left when the policeman arrived to take my statement. I explained that it was an accident and I didn't want to press charges. My mother had a hissy fit, "Officer, can we press charges for him?"

"I'm sorry ma'am, but your son is old enough to make his own decisions. If he says it was an accident, I have to believe him."

"No you don't! I watch the news. I've seen cases where some poor woman was being beaten by her husband and she didn't want to press charges but the city pressed charges anyway. I'm not stupid! I know there's something you can do to keep that boy away from my son."

"Ma'am, please calm down. Some areas do have laws about this sort of thing, unfortunately this is not one of those areas. If your son won't cooperate, there's nothing we can do."

"Stop talking about me like I'm not here. I am cooperating. It really was an accident," I told them. My mother, father and the policeman all gave me a look that told me they didn't believe me, but I also knew in my heart that Lionel wasn't trying to push me down the stairs. "I lost my balance and I fell. Okay? That's what happened so stop trying to make this in to a big deal."

"But it is a big deal," my mother said as she sat down next to me. I hated Henry and Michael for spilling their guts to her. They told her everything they had heard or seen and went to great lengths to describe various bruises I had.

My father felt compelled to speak. "What's wrong with you Luke? Being gay isn't good enough for you; you gotta go and be a fucking pansy as well? Grow some balls and be a man goddamnit! That boy hurt you and everyone in this room knows it, so just say it, so we can help you!"

"It was an accident."

My father looked at my mother and pointed to me. "See! You see this shit! I can't put up with it! You asked me to be nice to him and not hurt his precious little feelings because he's in a lot of pain and his heart is broken, but look at this piece of shit! Lionel put him in a goddamn hospital bed and he wants to sit here and defend that fucking boy. I bit my tongue when he woke up and asked all those questions about his little boyfriend, but I will not sit by quietly and watch this go down." My father looked at me. "Do you enjoy having the crap beat out of you? Is that it?" I couldn't respond. "We didn't raise you to be this way and I'm not going to stand here and watch you make an ass of yourself. Lionel doesn't love you! He probably never has. He's a sick bastard and you're an even sicker bastard for putting up with him. If you want him, fine, have him!" Then he looked me in my eyes. "You're even less of a man than I thought you were." He stormed out of the room. I lowered my head in shame. The policeman gave me his card and excused himself and my mother stayed in the room and held my hand as I battled with my thoughts.

I spent three days in the hospital paralyzed from the waist down and the fourth day I finally felt something. At first it was a passing surge of numbness or a slight tingle every now and then, so I didn't tell anyone because I was afraid that I was imagining the sensations. Then, about five days after I woke up, I felt my legs again. To say I was relieved would be an understatement. I couldn't imagine my life without basketball, which for some strange reason was my biggest complaint about possible paralysis, as if basketball was the only use I had for my legs.

My father didn't come back to see me but that didn't bother me. In fact, I preferred his absence because I didn't want to look in his eyes and see his disappointment. At least my mother seemed more sad for me than anything else and while her constant looks of pity made me want to scream, her presence made me feel better. Michael and Henry were in and out of my room, visiting whenever they could and giving me their own variations of my mother's look of pity. I stopped asking them about Lionel after the first day because they didn't seem very forthcoming with information and they made it clear that they didn't want to talk about him.

Troy and James from the basketball team came to see me. They gave me a ball autographed by the team and I found myself searching the ball for Lionel's name, but it wasn't there. I just wanted to touch something of his. Troy apologized for teasing me about my bruises. "I'm sorry man, I had no idea what was going on."

"It's okay," I told him.

"No, it's not, but I tell you what, when you get out of this place, I'll come to your dorm and wait on you. I can be your personal servant for a week."

"That's okay. I'm sure I can manage."

"No, I insist. I won't feel right until I make it up to you."

"Dude chill, he's obviously not interested in your help," James told him.

"I wasn't talking to you," Troy said then he turned his attention back to me. "So when are you getting out anyway?"

"I don't know. I just got feeling in my legs and the doctor is talking about rehab, but he said I'm young and healthy so I should be back on my feet in no time because nothing is broken. I'm hoping to play in our last home game."

"Is that realistic?"

"Probably not but I'll be happy to suit up and walk out on the court with you guys. Hopefully I'll be able to do that." I knew the NBA was definitely not in my future so any hope I had of basketball glory had to be achieved in college or abandoned forever.

"That's cool. Don't push yourself too hard though. I don't want you to get hurt trying to get back to us. We're going to need you next season."

"I won't rush, but I can't wait to get back. Basketball is my life."

"I thought Lionel was your life," quipped James.

"James!" Troy shouted.

"Sorry," James said.

"No, don't be sorry. You're right. Lionel meant a lot to me. He still does."

"What? The two of you are still together?" asked Troy.

"Not exactly. I know I can't be with him right now, but I still have hope. He's getting help and I don't know, maybe one day, who knows."

"He pushed you down a flight of stairs," Troy said before his eyes took on that look of pity I detested.

"Please don't look at me like that."

"Sorry, I'm not trying to. I don't pity you, if that's what you think. It's just that you seem like a great guy and I don't understand how you could be with someone who would treat you so bad. You deserve better."

"I know." I told him, finishing his sentence. "Don't you think I've heard it before?"

"Yeah man, I'm sure you have. It's none of my business anyway. Forget I said anything."

"We should leave," James said.

"Okay."

I was surprised when Troy walked over to me and gave me a hug. "I'm going to come back and check on you, so take care of yourself until I see you again, okay man?"

"Okay. Thanks for coming," I told them as they walked towards the door.

"No prob, dude," said James.

Michael and Henry were walking in as Troy and James walked out. "Damn Henry, he's replaced us already," Michael joked. James kept walking, but Troy stopped for a second and nodded at them before he walked out the door. They each gave me a hug and then pulled up a chair next to my bed.

"How are you feeling?" asked Henry.

"Much better. Today is the best I've felt all week."

"Yeah, you look better," said Michael. "I guess that's what happens when you get a visit from two cuties from the basketball team."

"Troy and James?"

"Yes!"

"What? I'm not looking at them like that. I'm surprised they're still talking to me now that everyone knows I'm gay."

"I'm not. You're a good basketball player and they need you. We're all mature adults now, right?"

"Speak for yourself," said Henry. We laughed.

After the laughter subsided, Michael started talking, "I wouldn't be surprised if that Troy had a crush on a certain someone in this room."

"Who?" I asked.

"Who do you think?"

"Me? No way! He just feels bad about teasing me about my bruises."

"Right, that's why he blushed when he was leaving."

"You made him uncomfortable. Many people blush when they're uncomfortable. That doesn't prove anything."

"How long did they stay?"

"Not you too Henry! They didn't stay that long. They came in and gave me this ball, then Troy apologized about some comments he made and they left."

"What did he say when he apologized?" asked Michael. I could hear the excitement in his voice.

"He offered to be my personal servant for a week to make it up to me."

"Oooh," they said in unison.

"Stop it, you guys! You know I'm still holding out for Lionel."

Their smiles faded and I could feel the happiness empty the room and leave only their judgments behind. "Lucas, you can't mean that."

I regretted opening my big mouth. "Look guys I know how you feel about him and you know how I feel about him. I didn't mean to bring it up so let's just pretend I didn't."

"We're going to have to talk about it eventually," Henry said.

"Well will one of you at least tell me what happened to him? Where is he? Why hasn't he called me or come to visit?"

"He was out on bail, but thanks to you refusing to file charges, the case was dropped and he's a free man. He's back on the basketball team acting as if nothing happened. I heard the coach is making him do anger management in addition to the therapy, but I don't know. As to why he hasn't called you or come to visit, I'm sure he knows better than to show his face around here again. He came to see you right after he posted bail and your mother lit in to him pretty good. She made it clear that he wasn't welcome here and he had better leave you alone. Then she had the police escort him away. It was a little scary at the time but looking back, it was pretty funny. You should have seen the two little guys who drug him out of here."

"How did he look when you saw him? Did he look okay?"

"He looked fine and that's all I care to say about him, so let's drop the subject."

"Henry, come on."

"I told you what you've been dying to know since you opened your eyes, what more do you want from me?"

"I don't know. I want to talk about him. I miss him. I can't be with him and I don't want to be with him right now, but that's not going to erase him from my mind. I want to know what he's doing and how he's feeling. Is his therapy helping? Things like that."

"Do you want to see him?"

I felt shame as I answered, "Yes," but truthfully I did want to see him. Although, I only wanted to see him from a distance because I didn't want him to see me; I wasn't ready to look him in his eyes yet.

"You've got to be kidding me!" yelled Michael.

"Mike, calm down, I got this," Henry told him. "I tell you what Lucas. You want to know how Lionel's doing and I want to make sure you're okay. So how about I check on Lionel for you and tell you how he's doing, if you promise to leave him alone for the time it takes you to rehab in here because talking to him may delay your progress. You don't need to deal with the stress he brings, but at the same time, I know you'll drive yourself crazy if you don't know what's going on with him. So what do you think?"

I had to admit that his plan sounded good. I wanted to put off direct communication with Lionel until I had more time to think and Henry was offering me the perfect arrangement. I tried not to smile when I said, "Sounds fair to me."

"I mean it though. No contact with him at all. Can you promise me that?"

"I guess so."

"Don't guess, know."

"Okay. I won't talk to him until I'm better."

"Not even if he calls?"

"Not even if he calls. I'll tell him I have to focus on me right now and he should focus on him."

"That sounds really good."

"No it doesn't! Henry what's wrong with you? He needs to cut off everything with Lionel. He shouldn't care if he's alive or dead after what that jackass did to him."

"Michael shut up. Would you rather Lucas talk directly with him? Is that what you want, because that's what's going to happen if one of us doesn't suck it up and do it! I agree he shouldn't have anything to do with Lionel, but he doesn't realize that yet and this is the best alternative I can come up with."

I was surprised that Henry would reveal his plan with me sitting right there. "So that's the master plan, huh?"

"What?" asked Henry.

"You want to serve as our mediator so you can monitor our discussions and hopefully drive us apart?"

"I'm not going to drive you apart. I'm sure Lionel can do that without my help. Your time away from him can only give you a little clarity about your situation."

"You got it all figured out, don't you?"

"I like to think I do," he said with a smile returning to his face.

"Okay, you got me. I'm not talking to Lionel any time soon. I promise." The rest of our conversation was Lionel-free and after a while, the tension left over from talking about him was gone.

My mother stopped by for a few minutes before visiting hours were over. She made another excuse for my father's absence and I played along even though we both knew why he wasn't there.

After she left, I was alone with my thoughts. My first thoughts were about Lionel, but then I thought about my day. I found myself thinking about Troy. He was 6'3" and similar in build to Lionel. His eyes were a light hazel color that contrasted with his honey brown skin tone. His wavy black hair was usually cut so short that you couldn't see the waves, but he had been growing it out lately and getting it braided and now it was a little past his ears. It wasn't braided when he came to visit me and I remembered him tucking some of his hair behind his ear while he talked to me. I had to admit that it was kind of cute. I closed my eyes as I thought about Troy but I went to sleep with Lionel as my final conscious thought.

I woke up the next morning with flowers sitting next to me and a note. I opened the note and it read, "Hey Lucas, I heard you woke up. I miss you and I'm sorry. Call me. Lionel"

I had just enough time to smell the flowers before Henry walked in. "Ooh, who sent you flowers?" he asked. Before I could respond, he picked up the note and read it. Then he took the note and the flowers and put them in the trash.

"Why'd you do that?" I asked.

"No contact, remember?"

Chapter 21

He's Not Lionel

Rehabilitation was kicking my ass but my friends were making it a little better. Lionel was sending me flowers all the time with notes attached. Henry managed to intercept a few of them, but I was able to keep most of the notes by hiding them in my drawer with all the cards from well-wishers. My mother tried to convince me to go to the hospital near our home, but I wanted to stay close to campus and to a certain degree, close to Lionel. Henry was only telling me basic information and refused to pass any messages directly between me and Lionel. I tried to get a couple of the guys on the basketball team to give Lionel a message from me, but they all refused. I called Lionel a few times, but I couldn't find the words to speak to him, so I hung up after he answered the phone. The truth was that I just wanted to hear his voice.

I was sitting in my hospital room preparing to embark on my return to college. I had my clothes on and a smile on my face when Troy walked in.

"Why are you smiling?" he asked.

"I'm going home today."

"No you're not. You're going to Michael's apartment. Your home is thousands of miles away."

"Don't try to be funny, Troy."

"Okay, a smile on your face and testy at the same time. Are you ever going to be easy to read?"

"I've never been easy," I teased.

He looked to the side like he was thinking and then he said, "Well, that's true. I've been trying to get in your pants for two months now and you still won't give me any play." I knew I was blushing. He reached with his left hand and stroked my cheek. "Stop blushing."

"I'm not blushing."

"Yes you are. You can't even deny it, but don't worry," he leaned down to my ear and whispered, "I won't tell anyone."

A tingle went through me. He always flirted with me and I tried my hardest not to flirt back and lead him on, but sometimes I wondered why I was fighting it so hard. I couldn't think of a good reason not to give him a chance. The only thing holding me back was the hope that Lionel would somehow be fixed and we would get together and be happy, but I found myself losing a little hope each day.

"Stop hitting on me," I told Troy as I pushed him away.

"You know you love it," he said then he pushed me back on my hospital bed and climbed on top of me.

I knew I should push him away, but I missed intimate contact so I let him stay there for a few seconds. "Ouch you're hurting me," I said.

"No I'm not. The doctor said you're mostly healed. The only hurt you're feeling is that hardon in your pants." He ground in to me. "And I can help you with that if you let me."

I laughed. It came out a little girly, but I was nervous. He laughed with me and then he abruptly stopped laughing. We were face to face and I knew what he was about to do, but the only thought running through my mind was that I was about to let him do it. His face came closer to mine and then our lips made contact. All of his flirtations and all of my denials crashed together and as his tongue pushed in to my mouth, I knew he had won. I kissed him back without intending to. After a few seconds, I gave up my mental battle and gave in to the physical pleasure. I put my hands under his shirt and rubbed his bare skin and he started moaning in to my mouth as he pressed in to me.

Someone whistled and I pushed Troy away. We both looked over and Michael and Henry were standing in the doorway. "Looks like we're interrupting," Henry said.

"Shut up," I told him as I sat up.

Michael glared at Troy. "So how's it going Troy?"

I looked at Troy and he blushed. "Everything is great Mikey. In fact everything is better than I expected." He turned to me and smiled.

"How many times do I have to tell you, it's Michael or Mike, but never Mikey!"

"Aww, come on Mikey, lighten up," Troy said. He and Michael had an interesting relationship and I still wasn't sure what was going on with them. Henry said they were both being bitches to each other because they both wanted me.

"Whatever Trevor." Michael rolled his eyes and looked at me. "So I see you're ready to go. Did the doctor sign your discharge papers yet?"

"No, I'm supposed to tell the nurse when you get here so he can give me the forms."

"I'll go tell him," Henry said, turning around in a hurry. The rest of us all smiled. We knew Henry had a thing for the nurse. I tried to explain to him that the nurse wasn't gay, but he told me I was wrong and he had relentlessly pursued the nurse since the first day he saw him. I had to admit the nurse did seem to smile more when Henry was around but I couldn't tell if it was because he was flattered or because he was interested.

"When are those two going to get together?" Michael asked.

"They're not," I told him.

"How much do you want to bet?"

"Dessert for a week?"

"You're going to be dessert for a week? Is that your offer?"

"Stop playing. I meant I'll make us dessert for a week if I lose and you can do dessert for a week if I win."

"Oh, okay. I guess that could work, too. How long is this bet for because I don't want to give Henry too long."

"How about a month? Henry should move on by then."

"Move on to who?" Troy asked.

"Some girl, some guy, who knows with him, he likes them both."

"He's bisexual?" Troy asked in surprise.

"I thought you knew that," I said.

"No, he always struck me as just gay."

"Well he's not."

"Why do you care, anyway?" Michael questioned as his eyes threw daggers at Troy.

"I don't. I was just asking," Troy responded.

"Whatever," Michael said.

"Whatever, yourself," Troy told him in an irritated voice.

"Okay you two," I warned. They both seemed to back down and neither said anything else. I wondered how Michael and Troy were going to get along once I was in Michael's apartment. I kept telling Troy he didn't have to wait on me for a week, but he insisted and he managed to convince Michael to let him move in for a week so he could make sure all of my needs were met. Personally, I thought Troy either paid Mike or threatened him, but I wasn't sure which one.

Henry walked in with the nurse behind him. I signed my discharge papers and spoke to the nurse about my medications then I was in the passenger seat of Michael's new car and Troy and Henry were in the backseat.

"I can't believe your parents didn't come back to see you released from the hospital," Michael said.

"My mother is still pissed that I didn't go back there and my father, well, you know how he feels about this situation. He didn't even say goodbye to me before they left, but what more can I expect from him? At least he was honest about how he felt."

"I was honest about how I feel," he glanced at me, "about your fascination with Lionel, but I'm still here supporting you. There's no excuse for him abandoning you and forcing your mother to go back home when she wanted to stay here and take care of you."

"She didn't want to stay here. She wanted to take care of me at home," I corrected him.

"She would have stayed if he didn't push her. You should have seen the argument they had in the lobby."

"I definitely wouldn't have wanted to see that," I told him as I bit my lower lip and looked out the window. I closed my eyes and prayed that the tears wouldn't fall and luckily, they didn't, but the pain jabbed at my heart. I wanted my parents to be with me through my rehabilitation and my release, but my father had other plans.

We got to Michael's apartment and they led me to the bedroom. I smiled when I saw that Michael and Henry had brought a lot of my things. "Your clothes are in the top two drawers and in the closet," Henry told me. "We grabbed as much stuff as we could while Lionel was at practice."

"Don't say that name here," Michael warned.

"Sorry, I forgot. Should I call him 'he who must not be named?'"

Michael laughed then he said, "No, that's wasting too many breaths on him and we all know he's not worth it."

Michael and Henry laughed together and I ignored them. Troy interrupted them when he said, "I have to go get my clothes and my sleeping bag. I'll be back in about an hour."

"No need to rush," Michael told him. Troy winked at him and then left. "I don't know why you spend so much time with him, Lucas. He's so annoying."

"He's not that bad."

"Is that why you were kissing him?" Michael asked.

"I was wondering when you were going to get to that," Henry told him. Then Henry turned his attention to me, "So why were you making out with him on your hospital bed? How long have the two of you been messing around?"

"We're not messing around. It just kind of happened, but it was nothing. You know where my heart is."

"It looked like your heart was trying to suck out Troy's," Henry said.

"I don't know how that happened. One second he was flirting with me, the next, he was shoving his tongue down my throat."

"Stop putting it on him, you liked it," Henry told me.

"I didn't like it," I protested, even though I knew I had enjoyed the kiss as much as any with Lionel, if not more. Troy seemed much gentler than Lionel and surer of himself.

"Yes you did," Henry teased.

"He said he didn't so just drop it," Michael said as he walked towards the bed. "So how are you feeling Lucas? Are you hungry?"

"I'm fine and I'm not hungry yet," I told him, "but thanks for asking."

"Are you thirsty?" he asked.

"I guess I could drink something."

"Okay, I'll go get you some water." Michael left the room and Henry sat on the bed next to me.

"You still don't think Michael's in love with you?"

"He's my friend."

"And? Does that mean he can't be in love with you?"

"Well I guess the two don't have to be mutually exclusive but he doesn't love me that way. He loves me like you love your dog or your mom."

"You don't dream about kissing your dog or your mom. At least I hope not." He chuckled and I gave him a light push.

"I still say you're wrong."

"I'm right and I know it. I wish I could be a fly on the wall with the three of you here. It's going to be priceless."

"Don't start with me Henry."

"Okay, I won't, but I do have one question for you."

"What?"

"How did you feel when you were kissing Troy? And don't say you didn't feel anything because I know you felt something."

"I didn't feel anything," I told him.

"Yes you did. The sexual tension between the two of you has been getting thicker for weeks now."

"There is no sexual tension. We kissed and that's it."

"So you don't want to kiss him again?"

I smiled, "I didn't say that."

"You do, don't you?"

"I don't know, maybe. It did feel kind of nice."

"Good for you," he said.

"What's good for him?" Michael asked as he walked in with a glass of water.

"You didn't offer me anything to drink," Henry said.

"You know where the kitchen is," Michael told him. "Now what are the two of you talking about? What's good for Lucas?"

"Troy," Henry responded.

"Troy? What because they kissed? That's nothing. Lucas and I have done much more than that."

"Okay, Michael, that's nice." Henry's tone was patronizing, but Michael ignored him and handed me the water.

Michael quickly changed the subject and we played a few card games until Troy came back with his clothes, pizzas and movies. The pizza tasted great, but the company was even better. I was really enjoying hanging out with all of the guys but I found myself being drawn to Troy. I went to bed early and Troy was even in my dreams. I woke up the next morning and Troy was on the floor while Michael was in the bed with me. I imagined Troy was the person cuddled up behind me. I wondered if I was ready to move on with anyone, then I thought about Lionel and realized he wasn't the person I wanted to hold me anymore. I closed my eyes and cried as I worried what that revelation meant for our relationship.

Chapter 22

The Unexplainable

Troy and Mike bickered like two children and it drove me crazy. After three days trapped in an apartment with them, I told them I was going for a walk.

"Wait a second, I'll come with you," Troy said.

"No thank you, I want to be alone."

"Is that a good idea?" Michael asked.

"I won't be gone for long. You guys can argue over who gets to come find me if I'm not back in an hour." I opened the door and walked out, not waiting for a response.

I felt strange as I stepped out the front door of the building by myself. I took a deep breath to inhale the smell of fresh, unrestricted air. I was about to turn to the right and walk towards campus, but something caught my eye. Standing against the building across the street was a surprisingly clean cut looking Lionel. I froze when our eyes made contact. Everything inside me told me to run back in the building because I wasn't ready. I pleaded with my body to stop staring and move, but I felt cemented to the sidewalk. Lionel was halfway across the street when I realized his eyes were getting closer. He walked in front of me and my chance to escape vanished. He moved to put his arms around me and I backed away from him.

"I'm sorry," he said, "I'm just happy to see you."

"Why are you here?"

"I had to see for myself that you were alright."

"How did you know I was here?"

"I heard Troy saying he was moving in with Michael for a week so he could take care of you."

"Oh."

"Is he your boyfriend now?"

"Who?"

"Troy. He talks about you all the time and I can tell he wants to replace me."

"My personal life is no longer any of your business."

I expected him to get upset with me, instead, he said, "You're right. I'm sorry."

I gathered my composure and pushed away the images of a fragile Lionel who needed me and I tried to get away from him before the old feelings reclaimed their throne in my heart. "I guess I'll see you around." I turned to leave, but he grabbed my arm.

"Let me take you out to lunch."

"I'm not hungry."

"Well we can go get some coffee and talk. I'm not asking you to come back to me. All I'm asking for is a chance to talk to you." He quickly added, "Please."

"You know I don't drink coffee."

"Fine. Hot chocolate then."

"I don't think I can handle that."

"Why not?"

"It's too much."

"Okay, may I at least walk with you for a few minutes?"

"No. Just go away. I don't want to talk to you right now!" His grip on my arm tightened. "You haven't changed at all!" I told him.

He let go. "I just want to talk to you. I've been waiting out here all damn day just to get a good look at you." He surprised me when he lowered his eyes to the ground between us and said, "I'm sorry. I understand if you're not ready and I accept your decision. My number hasn't changed so call me when you're ready."

He turned to walk away and I rashly yelled, "Wait!" When he turned back around, his face had hope scribbled all over it. "Do you want to go to dinner?" I asked before I was able to think clearly.

"I'd love to."

"Okay. Be back here at 7 and we'll go out and talk." His smile warmed me on the inside and I cursed myself for my weakness. "We're just going to talk, that's all, stop smiling. I need closure so I can move on with my life, without you." His smile slithered away and I felt a twinge of pride at being able to make it disappear.

"I'll see you at 7."

"Okay." I ran back in the building, flustered and confused. My heart was thumping in my chest and I was having a hard time breathing. I didn't understand why I would agree to see him so soon. He did look good though and that thought only made me curse myself and him. Damn him for being so fine. It wasn't fair. A torrent of emotions and memories shattered my body. I was trying to move forward but at the same time I was being sucked back in to the old feelings I had for Lionel. As much as I hated him, I still hoped we could at least salvage a friendship from the wreckage of our relationship.

I walked in Michael's apartment and he and Troy seemed surprised that I was back so soon. "That was quick," Michael said.

"I ran in to Lionel."

"What? Tell me you didn't talk to him."

"I had no choice, my feet wouldn't move. I told him we can go to dinner tonight and talk."

"What do you have left to say to him? Thanks for almost killing me!"

"Michael, don't be so dramatic. I don't want to be with him anymore, but that doesn't mean I can't talk to him. In fact, I think I need to talk to him. I need to make him understand that I'm never going to let him hurt me again."

"You can do that by staying away from him."

Troy decided to join the conversation. "Michael, why don't you shut up? Lucas can do whatever he wants to do and if he wants to go see that asshole then let him. It might be good for him."

"How can you support him when you know how much Lionel hurt him? Both of you are ridiculous! I'm going to go talk to some people who actually use their brains!" He grabbed his keys in dramatic fashion, brushed by me and stormed out, yelling, "Don't wait up!"

Troy shook his head. I felt guilty. I said, "I didn't mean to upset him."

"He hates Lionel. Just hearing that name upsets him." Troy smiled and I walked over and sat next to him.

"Thanks for understanding."

"I'm not sure that I do understand, but it's your choice."

"Will you come with me?"

"Tonight?"

"Yes. I need someone to be there with me. I don't trust myself alone with him."

"Do you trust yourself alone with me?" Troy asked with a devilish grin.

Some signals crossed in my head and I felt the need to prove to myself that I was over Lionel. "No." I leaned forward and kissed him. I had a flash that he was Lionel and I pulled back. "I shouldn't have done that."

"Yes you should." He kissed me and put his hand on my thigh. I tried to relax under his touch as his hand inched up my thigh and sent sexual sensations running through my body. He moved from my mouth to my chin and then to my neck. His soft lips felt good as they grazed my flesh. His fingers undid the buttons on my shirt and I moaned when his warm hand rubbed against my bare skin.

I sighed when his tender kisses stopped. He grabbed my hand and led me to Michael's bedroom. A thrill went through my body when I thought we were going to do something on Michael's bed, but Troy sat down on his sleeping bag and motioned for me to sit next to him. I had a second to think about what was going on and I said, "Maybe this isn't a good idea." I knew I was doing it for all the wrong reasons.

Troy stood up and walked towards me. He dropped to his knees in front of me and looked in to my eyes. He licked his lips seductively and then reached for my belt buckle. He must have been afraid that I would try to stop him if he didn't act quickly because he had my pants around my ankles in less than a second. He smiled when he saw I wasn't wearing underwear. I hadn't felt like putting any on.

His hand grabbed my dick and stroked it a few times before he put the head in his mouth and alternated between swirling his tongue and sucking. The variation was driving me crazy. He let my dick fall out of his mouth, but his hand kept it pointing at his lips. He kissed the tip. He kissed his way down the shaft, moving his hand out of the way. He kissed his way back up, letting his tongue slip out and leave a wet trail. His hand returned to stroking me and soon his mouth had swallowed the head again. He began slowly taking more of my dick until it had completely disappeared in his mouth. He didn't do that for long.

"I don't want you to cum yet," he explained. He licked each of my balls and then sucked on them for a few minutes. He put one of his fingers in his mouth and then he took it out and held it up for me. I leaned down and enveloped the finger with my lips trying to taste what he tasted. I stared in to his eyes and felt intoxicated by the pure lust I saw staring back at me. He pulled his finger out of my mouth and placed it against my hole, applying a little pressure. His finger pushed inside me with only our saliva as lubrication and it was slightly painful considering nothing had been up there in months, but the pain subsided as he slowly pushed inside me. His finger explored until he felt my prostate, then he took my dick in his mouth again and worked up a nice rhythm while his finger stimulated my prostate in unison with his head bobbing on my dick. My knees felt weak from the pleasure my body was feeling. Troy stopped his rhythm as he guided me to his sleeping bag but he didn't take my dick out of his mouth or his finger out of my ass.

The image of my dick lost in his mouth made my dick twitch. Troy felt it and pulled off. "Not yet," he said.

He took his finger out of me and pulled me down on the bag. He had me lay on my back and he was about to push my legs open when I told him, "Take off your clothes."

He looked disappointed that I was interrupting the moment, but I wanted to see him naked before we went any further. Instead of ripping off his clothes, Troy stood up and slowly took his shirt off. I tried to take a picture of all the parts of him I hadn't noticed before. The best word to describe his nipples was juicy. They were juicy, plump, and tantalizing. He squeezed his nipples with his fingers and then he let his hands glide down over his abs. His hands went lower and lower until they were inside his pants playing with the object of my desire. He was teasing me, but I was impatient, I wanted him to fuck me and get it over with. I got off the bag and practically ripped the rest of his clothes off. He smiled at my eagerness.

"Lay down," he ordered. I did and he got on the bag and lifted my legs. I thought he was going to put his finger back inside me, but he lowered his head to my hole and started licking it. I moaned as waves of pleasure began to overtake me again. He put his finger back in my ass and he quickly followed that by adding another finger, then another. I arched my back and moaned my appreciation with my eyes closed. He went down on my dick and I was beginning to think that he was obsessed with sucking it but I got distracted by the stars I was starting to see. His attack went on for only a few seconds and then he licked and kissed his way up my body to my left nipple. He licked it with his tongue and my moaning got louder. "I want you," he whispered. When his movement stopped, I opened my eyes and looked down. He was staring at me. "Can I have you?" he asked. His eyes, like my body, pleaded with me to say, yes.

"Yes." I almost screamed. He got up and unzipped the side pocket on one of his bags.

He ripped the condom open and put it on then got on top of me. He grunted as my ring gave way and let him in. He was slow and deliberate with every move he made but he sped up as he approached his climax. I was the first to cum, shooting between us, and he came a few seconds later with a loud growl. He was good and definitely better than Lionel. He kissed me and I kissed him back until my mind caught up to what had just happened, then I turned my face to the side. He moved and sat down next to me.

I felt ashamed of what I had done. I knew I wasn't ready for a relationship with Troy. What happened between us was purely physical because I needed some form of release after seeing Lionel. I used Troy. It was not my intention to do that, but I did. "I'm sorry," I told him.

"Don't be, I know your heart wasn't in it." He kissed my cheek. "Maybe next time, I'll be the one you want." I could tell he was hurt, but he managed to smile at me. "I'm going to go take a shower."

"Alright." While he was in the shower I thought about my stupid impulsive behavior and I cried silent tears. I knew Troy really cared about me and I had taken advantage of that.

Troy came back and I left to take my own shower. When I returned to the room, Troy and his sleeping bag were gone. I thought I had chased him away. I put on some clothes and walked out to the living room. My heart nearly stopped when I saw Troy sitting on the sofa.

"I thought you were gone."

"I put my sleeping bag in the washer."

"Oh."

"You want to talk about it?" he asked.

"No."

"Okay. You want to watch TV with me?"

"Sure." I put a pillow on the floor and sat on it because I didn't want to sit near him.

"You still want me to go with you tonight?"

"If you want to."

"Do you want me to?"

"Yes." We made small talk after that but the conversation was strained. At 6:30 we got up and put on decent clothes. We waited until 7:10 to go meet Lionel.

Lionel was standing next to the building's entrance. His face lit up when he saw me, but immediately fell when he saw Troy walk out behind me. "What the hell is he doing here?"

"I asked Troy to come with me."

"Why? You don't need a bodyguard. I'm not going to hurt you."

"I can't be alone with you."

"I can't say what I need to say in front of him. He wouldn't understand."

"So you don't want to go to dinner?"

"I don't want to sit across from that punk."

"Fine. I'll see you around campus." I turned to walk away but Lionel stopped me.

"No, no. He can come."

"So where are we going to eat?"

"Wherever you want, my treat." He looked over my shoulder, "You have to pay for yourself though." Troy didn't say anything.

"How about the steakhouse down the street?"

"Okay."

We walked three blocks to the steakhouse and sat at a booth in the middle of the restaurant. I was sitting next to Troy and Lionel was sitting across from us with his eyes glued to my every move. We made it halfway through dinner without speaking.

"You know I loved you, don't you?" Lionel asked. "I still love you."

"I know Lionel, I know." I kept eating almost ignoring him.

"Do you think we can ever be friends again? I mean I know I fucked up but I miss you every day. I was wrong for everything I did to you and I'm sorry. I know that won't make it better, but I am. You didn't deserve to be treated like that. I was such an asshole."

Troy threw his fork down on his plate. "It's starting to stink to high hell over here."

"If you have something to say to me, say it!" Lionel yelled at him.

"That's okay Lionel. I think you're doing a good job on your own. Just one correction though," Troy leaned forward and said, "You're still an asshole." He sat back in the booth and was quiet for the rest of dinner.

Lionel kept telling me that he had changed and I believed him. The old Lionel would have kicked my ass and Troy's, but the new Lionel clenched his teeth and smiled. The new Lionel didn't bark at me for ignoring him or not responding fast enough. The new Lionel gave me all the time I needed to gather my thoughts. Dinner was almost over when I told him, "The answer is yes."

"Yes to what?"

"I think we can be friends again, but I know it's going to take a lot of work."

"I'm willing to work as hard as I need to." He was digging in his wallet for the money when he asked, "Does this mean you forgive me?"

"I forgave you already, but I can't forget what you did to me. That is why things will never be the same between us."

"Fair enough." After the bill was paid, Lionel walked with us to Michael's building. When we reached the door, he asked, "So when are we going to hang out again? Minus the shadow of course."

"I don't think I'll be ready to hang out with you any time soon." I realized at dinner that things were going too fast and I never should have agreed to go to dinner in the first place. One second I saw my old friend then I'd look across the table again and I'd see a monster. I needed more time.

"Okay, you're in control, so whatever you want, just let me know." He pulled me in to a hug before I realized what was happening. I stiffened under his touch and I felt everything in me turn cold. He released me and commented, "You never used to freeze like that. Is it because of me?"

"Don't ever touch me," I barked.

"Sorry."

"Stop apologizing for everything!"

"Sorry," he replied before he realized his mistake. "I didn't mean that I um"

"Please leave."

"For good?"

"No, just for now." I should have left it at that, but I added, "I'm tired of being near you." I knew I was trying to upset him.

He surprised me when he remained calm. "Okay. Goodnight Lucas." He shot a glare at Troy and then Lionel walked down the street.

Troy and I were sitting on the sofa when Troy said, "You still love him don't you?"

"What?"

"I could see it when you looked at him, and don't get me started on the way you treated him."

"I don't love him anymore."

"You don't want to love him anymore, but you still do. Do you think you'll ever get back together with him?"

"No, I can't get over what he did to me." That was the only thing I knew for sure.

"So when are you going to let him go?"

"I don't know. Maybe after two more chaperoned dates." I smiled at Troy and he laughed a little. "I really am trying to let him go, but it's hard. I spent a long time wanting him."

"You don't have to explain yourself to me. I just wanted to know if I had a real chance."

"Well what do you think?"

"I'll let you know when I figure it out."

"Okay, you do that then."

I was relieved that the awkwardness that had hung over us after our midday encounter dissipated in to our usual friendly banter. By the time Michael made it back, Troy and I were okay with each other again. We heard Michael drop his keys in the hallway and laugh like a hyena before he opened the door and saw the two of us sitting on the sofa.

"How was dinner with the devil?" he asked.

Chapter 23

There's Always More

I didn't have to tell Henry the Lionel story because Michael beat me to it. I woke up the morning after I went to dinner with Lionel, and Michael and Henry were in the living room chatting away.

I was still groggy when I walked out and saw them. "What are you guys gossiping about?" I asked.

Henry looked disappointed. "I can't believe you went to dinner with Lionel. I thought we agreed that you wouldn't talk directly to him."

"He was waiting for me when I went outside and"

"So he's stalking you now?"

"He wasn't stalking me. He knew I was here and he wanted to talk to me so he stood outside and waited."

"Was he going to stand outside all day?"

"I don't know. He sure as hell wasn't going to knock on the door." I felt like they were attacking me.

"Don't look at me like that." Michael said.

"Like what?" I asked. My mind went to Lionel.

"Like it's my fault. I don't like him and he's not welcome here."

"Why are you guys trying to control my life? I can make my own decisions."

Michael spoke, "Nobody said you couldn't."

"Michael, didn't we have this argument last night?"

"Yes and you still don't get it."

I sighed. "I'm going back to bed." I turned and walked back to the bedroom.

"Come back and talk to me," Henry said.

"I'll talk to you later." I shut the bedroom door and lied down on the floor next to Troy.

"What's going on?" Troy asked as he put his arm around me.

"Michael and Henry were attacking me about going to dinner with Lionel. They think I shouldn't see him at all."

"Yeah, I think Michael made that clear last night."

I laughed picturing Michael's hysterics from the night before. "Yeah, he did." Troy pushed his sleeping bag open and I cuddled up next to him. He kissed my neck and rubbed my arm as I fell asleep.

Henry woke me up a little while later and talked to me about seeing Lionel. He wasn't as judgmental as Michael, but I could tell he was far from pleased. He wanted me to be careful and he asked a lot of questions. Troy interrupted a few times and shared his opinion but he tried to stay out of it.

Over the rest of the week, I tried to figure out why I couldn't just be with Troy and be happy. My mind knew I should but my heart was still confused.

Michael and I attempted to talk about Lionel one more time. Michael said I was crazy to still love Lionel. I tried to explain to him that I would always love Lionel but that didn't mean I was dumb enough to go back with him. There was a lot of shouting. Michael and I decided not to talk about Lionel again because we weren't able to have a civil discussion when Lionel was concerned.

Troy moved out of the apartment after his week of servitude. He didn't want to go but Michael left him no other choice. I was sad to see Troy leave but I had to admit that I was relieved to have the constant bickering end. Living with Troy and Michael was stressful and I had enough things on my plate without adding them to the mix.

Troy came to Michael's apartment early Monday morning so he could walk me to campus. He and Michael had an argument about who should walk me and I let them know that both of them could walk with me at the same time.

I felt strange when we reached campus. "Am I imagining that everyone is staring at me?" I asked Michael.

"Yes. No one is looking at you."

"Yeah, you're not that popular," Troy joked.

I flashed a smile and kept walking even though my stomach was filled with butterflies. I hadn't set foot on campus since I fell down the stairs. A few guys from the basketball team saw us and came over to speak to me and tell me that they were looking forward to me coming back next season. One of the guys told me they were giving Lionel a hard time because of what he had done to me and I wondered why Troy hadn't mentioned anything.

I couldn't stop the feeling of sadness I had for Lionel. "Don't be too hard on him," I blurted out. Everyone looked confused. "He didn't mean to hurt me."

Michael threw his arms in the air, sighed loudly and walked away. "What's wrong with him?" asked one of the guys.

"He and I see the situation differently."

"Oh."

"Lucas needs to get to class so he'll have to give you the play by play later," Troy said as he grabbed my arm and pulled me away from the guys. We reached the building of my first class and I stopped. "Are you okay?"

"I'm fine. It's just. Well. You don't have to walk me to the door. I'm a big boy. I think I can handle it from here."

He laughed. "I don't mind. In fact, I'm not doing this for you; I'm doing this for me. I want to make sure you make it to your class and I'm going to worry about it unless I see it for myself."

"Worry about what? Me running in to Lionel?" I smiled, but he didn't. "Oh my goodness, that's what you're worried about. What do you think Lionel is going to do to me?"

"It's not that. It's more about how you're going to react if you see him."

"You don't have to worry. I'll be fine if I see him. I've seen him before." I waved at him. "You can leave now." I took one step forward and then I heard someone calling our names. I turned around and saw James running in our direction. James stopped next to me.

He looked at Troy then back at me. "So what's going on with you two?"

"Nothing," Troy quickly replied. "We're just friends. I mean you know he's had a hard time with Lionel and I just"

"Troy I'm fucking with you. I already know what's going on." I had to look at him closer when he said that because I could hear in his voice that he meant he knew for certain what was going on. "So how are you feeling Lucas? You all healed up?"

"For the most part."

"Yeah, I know what you mean. It's not easy to mend a broken heart."

"He didn't say that," Troy told him.

"He didn't have to." James put his hand on my shoulder. "I know we're not close, but you can always talk to me if you need to." He looked at Troy. "I'm good at keeping secrets. Ask Troy."

"Really?" I gave Troy a questioning look and Troy blushed.

"We'll have to talk to you later. Lucas doesn't want to be late for his class." Troy walked by James. "Come on Lucas."

I said, "Bye James."

He replied, "Call me."

Once inside the building, I asked, "Was he hitting on me?"

"No, he's straight."

"Are you sure?"

"He's my best friend. I think he would tell me."

"Oh, so what was all that about?"

"He knows how I feel about you and he's stupid, he thinks we should all be friends."

"That's not stupid."

Troy walked me to the door of my class. He handed me a small envelope. "I'm going to be in class when you get out so I can't pick you up, but here's my room key. I'm in room 211 in Hudson Hall. I wrote that on a sheet of paper in there in case you forget. James is my roommate. He might be there I'm not sure, but it doesn't matter because he knows you may stop by so it's not an issue."

"Thanks."

"One more thing."

"What?"

"Where are we meeting for lunch?"

We made arrangements for lunch and he left. I walked in the classroom and introduced myself to the professor who was surprised to see me.

"I heard about your ordeal young man." He shuffled some papers. "The work you've sent in has been excellent. You're doing better than most of the students who have been in class every day."

"Really? I thought class participation was a big part of the grade?"

"I sent you extra work to make up for that and you've turned everything in and now you're here so I'm sure you'll be participating. I can't fathom a reason why you won't continue to excel in this class."

"I can. I have never studied as much as I did when I was in the hospital. It helped keep my mind off of where I was but now I'm having difficulty focusing on the work."

"Well whatever the case. I'm pleased to see you in class today and I hope you will continue to do well but if you feel you need some extra help, both of my teaching assistants have office hours. Now if you'll please take a seat, class will begin in a minute."

I took a seat in the front of the room. About halfway through class I got the feeling that I was being watched so I looked around. There was a preppy looking black guy a few rows back, staring at me. He didn't even look away when I caught him. I turned around and tried to listen to the professor but I was too busy going over scenarios about the mystery guy. I started to feel paranoid, which caused me to stay in my seat at the end of class and wait for the guy to leave. I walked out the door and the guy was waiting for me.

"You're Lucas Donnelly aren't you?"

"Yes."

"Will you talk to me for a few minutes?"

"About what?"

He pushed open a door and walked in to an empty classroom. "Something important." He sat down at a desk and motioned for me to sit next to him.

I was afraid of what he knew, but I wanted to deal with it and get it over with, so I sat down. "What have you heard about me?" I asked.

"I hear you're a wonderful person and you've been hurt by someone you trusted."

"Does everyone know?"

"I don't think so. I know because Jay told me."

"Lionel?"

"Oh, I forgot you called him that. He said he treated you like shit but he only did it because he loved you so much. You have to understand that he didn't know any better. He had a rough childhood and nobody ever showed him how to love. I mean he knows what he did was wrong and he is so sorry and he's miserable without you. I know I'm stepping out of line but would you please just call him. That's all I'm asking for: call him. You don't have to talk to him or anything, just say hi. He's in real bad shape and I'm scared for him. I can't watch him every minute of the day."

I stared at the guy trying to figure out who he was because I had never seen him with Lionel before. Something about him reminded me of Lionel though. They had similar facial features. His eyes and nose were shaped like Lionel's and his build was about the same. He was a few shades lighter than Lionel though. "Who the hell are you?" I asked out loud.

"Oh I'm sorry. I should have told you. My name is Jayvon, but you can call be Von. I'm Lionel's brother."

"Lionel doesn't have a brother."

"Yes he does. Our mother raised me here and I didn't get to see Lionel much, but we talked on the phone every now and then and I knew about our father and his stepmother and you, Lucas Donnelly."

"Lionel would have told me if he had a brother."

"Look I don't know why he didn't tell you about me because he told me all about you. He didn't come here to come over to my house and have dinner with us and pretend to be a good family, or to spend the weekend with us or to get to know me better. He came here to be with you because he couldn't imagine his life without you in it. You were the only bright spot he had."

"What about Ronnie?" I didn't particularly care about his answer I only wanted to know if he really knew as much as he claimed to know about Lionel.

"Ronnie scared the hell out of him. He didn't know anything about being a father."

"So he abandoned him with a pervert?"

"It isn't like that."

"Well what is it like then?"

"Lionel did the best he could do given the situation and now he's trying to fix things. If you would talk to him, you would know that he is trying to get his son away from that woman and he's going to move him here to live with us."

"Lionel left his son with her, there's no excuse for that."

"Lionel was fucked up. He could barely take care of himself and you wanted him to take care of a child! My mother offered to help him out when I told her he was in counseling, but before that he didn't have anyone to depend on besides you."

"Where was your mother when that woman was molesting him? Or when his father was beating him?"

"What was she going to do? She couldn't afford another mouth to feed and she didn't want Lionel to go in to foster care. She would have taken both of us if she could have, but she couldn't, so she left Lionel behind. She knew our father would smack him around a little bit but I don't think she ever thought her own sister would abuse him."

"Her sister?"

"His stepmother."

'So that's why she could pass for Lionel's mother,' I thought. "But that makes her his"

"Yes, she's his aunt. My mother just thinks she hit him, she doesn't know about the other things her sister did to him and Lionel doesn't want her to know either."

I sat back and appraised his outfit. He didn't look like he was doing too badly. "You don't look like you're starving," I told him, "She should have taken Lionel too. How could she leave him?"

"Don't be fooled by the clothes, my mother and I were struggling until a few years ago. Now she finally has her shit together and she has a good job and I'm working too. I got an academic scholarship here so we don't have to worry about that and Lionel is working so we have three incomes at the house."

"Lionel lives with you?"

"Yes. My mother made him move in with us after he was assaulted."

"Assaulted?"

"A group of guys beat him up a few weeks ago. He wasn't seriously hurt or anything but I think it brought back memories because he showed up at our doorstep in pretty bad shape. My mother didn't want him to be alone after that."

"Did he file charges?"

"No. He thought he deserved it for how he treated you. He's been real messed up since what happened between you guys. I hadn't seen him smile again until you went to dinner with him last week. His therapist says he's making progress but I don't see it. He seems worse to me."

"I'm sorry he's unhappy but I can't help him."

"Just call him, please. Let him hear your voice."

"I'll think about it." A student walked in the room and sat down and that made me wonder what Jayvon was doing at my school. "How old are you anyway?"

"Same age as Lionel, we're twins."

"You don't look like twins."

"Well we're not identical."

That somehow made the story worse. "So you mean to tell me that your mother picked you over Lionel, left him with a monster of a father, knew about it, but left him there anyway, then allowed her sister to abuse him for years and screw with his head even more, and she didn't do anything about it, and now Lionel is living with you like you're all some big happy fucking family?"

"It's more complicated than that. Come with me to my house so I can show you something." Jayvon said.

"I have a class in ten minutes."

"Skip it. I'm missing a class right now. You need to see what I'm going to show you."

"Not today." I grabbed my books and ran out of the room trying to escape him. Things started to make sense. I remembered times when Lionel would be gone for the whole weekend to some mystery place he never spoke about and now I knew where he had been. No wonder Lionel was petrified of me leaving him. His real mother had abandoned him in that hell hole. When he told me the lady in his house was his stepmother, I just assumed his real mother had died and given the circumstances I think I would have preferred it if she had. Lionel's words the night he told me about his abuse played in my ear: 'Is that enough for you, or do you want to hear some more, because I've got more. '

I never would have been able to guess he had so much more to tell. I just assumed the abuse was bad enough. My heart hurt thinking about how he must have felt as a child knowing that his twin brother had a life that could have easily been his and knowing that no one loved him enough to care what happened to him, not even his own mother. I bumped in to someone at the building's entrance. Of course it had to be Lionel.

"Hey Lucas."

"Hey."

"Why are you running?"

"I met your brother."

"I meant to tell you about him."

"It doesn't matter. You and I are not together anymore so it's none of my business."

"We're still friends though, right?"

"If we were, you wouldn't have to keep asking. I don't know what we are." I couldn't look at him without wanting to pull him in to a hug and cry for his lost childhood so I took off. I walked down the path and ignored Lionel calling me. I saw Troy a few students ahead talking to James. I ran and tapped him on the shoulder.

"What's up? How was your class?" he asked.

"It was good until the end."

"What happened?"

"I met Lionel's brother."

"Oh, you met Jayvon?"

"You knew about him?"

"Everybody does. He enrolled this semester."

James added, "He was the person who told the basketball team that Lionel had been attacked."

"You knew about that too!" I yelled at Troy.

He scowled at James and then said, "Yes."

"Why didn't you tell me?"

"I didn't think you needed to know."

"You're just like Michael and Henry!" I tried to contain my anger. "I'm going to class."

"But you don't have class right now."

"Thanks for memorizing my schedule!" Everyone was trying to control me, including Troy and that pissed me off. I was more than capable of making my own decisions and taking care of myself. I didn't need them to try to protect me or decide what I did and didn't need to know.

"I just"

"Save it!" I rushed off in a huff and went to the one place on campus where I felt safest: my old room. I walked in the room and found it completely barren. I hadn't given up my room assignment yet and it appeared neither had Lionel because no one had moved in. I closed the door and dropped to the floor so I could get out a good cry, but my cry was interrupted by a knock. I wiped my face and opened the door. Lionel was standing there.

"I followed you," he said before he stepped in the room, shut the door and locked it.

Chapter 24

Mixed Signals

"Get out of my way Lionel!"

"No. I'm not letting you out of this room until you talk to me."

"I don't want to talk to you."

"Yes you do." He leaned against the door and folded his arms. I wanted to charge him and knock him out of my way but that didn't work the first time I tried it and I assumed it wouldn't work the second time. Lionel outweighed and out-muscled me. I was one of the smallest guys on the basketball team.

I sat on my old mattress and sighed then I stared at the window and didn't say a word. I was even careful not to breathe too loudly.

"Fine, I'll start talking," he said. I glanced at him and then returned my gaze to the window. "You're the only person I ever allowed myself to love. When we were together, I wasn't afraid that you'd leave me because I knew you would never hurt me. Well, I thought you would never hurt me."

"That's what I used to think about you," I told him.

"I know. I can't explain why I did the things I did."

I put up my hand. "Just stop. We've already been over this."

"Okay. How about Jayvon? Is it okay if I tell you about him?"

"You don't have to."

"I want to. I want you to understand what happened." He took my silence as a signal to continue. "I didn't tell you about Von and my real mother because I thought you would see that as a reason to leave me."

"Why?" I asked him with my attention still focused on the window.

"Because if my own mother couldn't love me, how could you? Why would you want to? In high school, I thought you and the other guys might think less of me if you found out and then when we came here and I had you all the time, I didn't want to ruin it by telling you about them. I used to sneak off and see them sometimes. When I realized I loved you, I went there to talk to Von and he knocked some sense in to me. I wasted so much time being afraid of you. I was going to move out but Von told me to stay and see where things led. I never thought they would lead us here though."

"Here as in you holding me prisoner?"

"No, here as in us not being together because I hurt you. I never wanted to hurt you."

"But you did and more than once."

"And you know how fucking sorry I am for that shit."

"Yeah, I know how sorry you are but nothing is going to change what you did to me."

"Dammit! Can't we move past that?"

"It's easy for you to say that. You're not the one who had the shit beat out of him for months by the person you loved."

"And you're not the one who has to deal with the guilt of knowing that you are responsible for your unhappiness. I did all of this shit. I broke your heart. I broke mine. I caused you to leave me, not my mother, not Von, but me. I drove you away just like I did to everyone else who tried to love me, and I'll probably do that to my son. I shouldn't try to be in his life. I'll just hurt him."

"You'd rather leave him with her? You know what she'll do to him."

"I know."

I guess he was waiting for me to say something. After a few minutes with no words, I looked at Lionel and saw tears dripping down his face. My heart twitched. Without thinking, I ran to him and put my arms around him. He held me and put his head on my shoulder. I was reminded of how much I missed him, especially being so close to him and having his body against mine. I knew I was going to cry. Then I felt his head move and I saw what was coming before he did it.

My heart stopped beating when his lips brushed lightly against mine. I shook my head to signal for him to stop but he found my lips again and pressed insistently instead of gently. His tongue stabbed my lips, which opened for their own protection. I momentarily forgot I shouldn't be kissing him because his mouth felt so welcoming and familiar, like something I wanted and needed but wasn't ready to accept again.

The kiss ended slowly with four pecks that were progressively shorter. His eyes captured mine and he said, "I missed you."

He shouldn't have said that because it caused me to come crashing down. It was bad enough I was kissing him in my dreams, but to actually do it in real life was shameful. Did I have so little respect for myself?

"What's wrong?" Lionel asked.

I caught him off guard when I pushed him to the side, but he recovered quickly and was pulling me away from the door before I was able to open it.

"You still love me, don't you?" he asked.

"Of course, but we will never be together the way you want us to be."

"Are you sure?"

"I have to be."

"Don't you miss being together? I know I miss holding you and kissing you."

I missed it too. I missed us. I missed him. I missed everything, well except him hitting me, but I wasn't going to go back to the way we were. I wasn't going to be with him. I had to keep my promise to myself.

"This isn't going to happen," I stated.

He pulled my arm. "Sit and talk to me then."

"About what?"

"I don't care."

"Fine." I sat on my old bed and resumed my sullen retreat in to another zone. Lionel walked over and sat down next to me.

"I don't want things to stay like this," he said.

"Neither do I."

"So what do we do?"

"I don't know, but we can't be together. We're not good for each other."

"How can you say that? You're the best thing that ever happened to me and I'm trying to be a better person for you."

"You shouldn't do it for me. Do it for yourself because you deserve to get better and you have a little boy who's going to need you to be okay. Do it because" He interrupted me with a kiss. I stood up. "Stop doing that!"

"It felt right."

"I don't give a damn about how it felt! It's hard enough being in the same room with you with us just talking. I can't handle anything else. How clear do I need to make it?"

"I'm sorry. I didn't mean to"

"I know you didn't, but don't do it again."

"Okay." I sat down next to him and he asked, "Will you at least let me hold you?"

"I don't think that's such a good idea."

"Please. I promise I won't try anything. I just want to hold you."

I knew I should say no. I knew I should leave, but I wanted to stay with him and pretend we were fine again. I desperately wanted to feel his arms around me. I just wasn't sure if I could leave it at that. "Alright."

He lied down on the mattress and patted the spot next to him. My movements were intentionally tentative because I didn't want him to know how excited I was to cuddle with him again. I started feeling bad and regretting my decision when I felt his arm around me and his body pressed up behind me. I felt his dick as it swelled in his pants. "Sorry, I can't help it," he said before I had a chance to comment.

"It's okay. Just start talking again."

Lionel was talking about his time without me but I was fixated on the sensation of his hardon against my ass. I felt like I was going crazy because my head was shouting at me to get up and leave, but my heart and my body were telling me to stay. My body was even telling me to give in to how I was feeling. I was lost in my thoughts trying to rationalize my behavior but I realized there was no way to rationalize it. One day I didn't want Lionel to touch me, the next day all I wanted was to feel his body against mine.

I fell asleep while Lionel was talking and woke up to the sound of Lionel lightly snoring in my ear. I could feel his hot breath beating on my neck and his limp dick against my ass. His arm was around me and it felt nice. I tried to be still because I didn't want to wake him and I didn't want to ruin the moment. My eyes closed and I fell asleep again.

I woke up to the feel of lips tickling my neck with kisses and Lionel humping me from behind. I turned my head slightly to the side and Lionel began sucking on my neck. I laid there trying to convince myself to move but my body was content where it was.

"I love you," Lionel whispered in my ear as he took a second to blow hot air on my skin.

I moaned and cursed myself at the same time. I didn't want him to love me anymore because I didn't want to still love him, but the feel of his body and the heat between us overwhelmed my good sense. I started convincing myself that I should have sex with him one last time and it could be like goodbye sex or something. Just closure, that was all. I would have sex with him and then I would move on and put him behind me. Somehow it all started to make sense to me. I turned on my back.

Lionel didn't skip a beat as his lips dove on top of mine and I welcomed his kiss. The kiss was passionate and rough like our tongues were trying to fight each other for control of the situation. I finally gave up and let him finish taking charge because I knew he would win. He always did.

"You don't know how much I've missed you," Lionel said as his hand tore at my shirt. Within seconds, we were both ripping each other's clothes off as if we were in a rush. I think I really was in a rush though because I knew the more time we took to get down to business, the more time I would have to really think about what I was doing, and I didn't want to think about it. I just wanted to do it. "I need you so badly," Lionel whispered as his fingers began invading me.

My mind started flashing thoughts, warning me that 'I shouldn't be doing anything with him. I was going to regret it and I should stop before we went too far,' but my body was on a completely different page. My body wanted Lionel more than I'd ever wanted him before. It was almost like I needed to have him. I needed to feel him inside of me. I needed to be with him. I needed him. I hated to admit it to myself but I knew it was true. I needed Lionel. I didn't understand why, but I knew I could no longer deny it. I hated him for what he had done, but I couldn't hate him forever because I loved him too damn much.

"I can't wait any longer," he told me, snapping me out of my thoughts long enough to see the lust and desperation in his eyes. I knew he wanted me so badly that it hurt and oddly, I found the idea intoxicating.

He withdrew his fingers and I waited for him to penetrate me. He inched gently inside me, almost teasing me with the pleasure of being filled up. I moaned and he grunted. He pushed all the way inside me and gave me a kiss before he pulled back out and started fucking me. It felt like it lasted forever. I was trying to hold back because I wanted to prolong the experience since I had promised myself it wouldn't happen again. I didn't know why he was holding back, but I appreciated his effort. He would push in and out and get a good rhythm going then he would stop and take a break so he didn't cum, but he always kept his dick inside me.

"I love you," he panted between grunts. "I fucking love you."

I felt myself about to cum and suddenly realized I was moaning Lionel's name, "Lionel, oh, Lionel, oh, Lionel." I shut my mouth immediately to prevent myself from saying his name again, but my mouth wasn't closed for long because I opened it and let out a loud moan as I came.

"Yeah, cum on this dick," Lionel said as he continued to pump throughout my orgasm. I was coming down from my climax when I heard Lionel say, "Oh shit." I felt his dick expand and empty its contents deep inside me.

He leaned down and kissed me and to my surprise, I kissed him back. He kept his still hard dick in place and started pumping me again a few minutes later.

"What do you think you're doing?" I asked him.

"Giving you what you want," he replied before he kissed me again.

I wanted to stop him but my voice had been taken over by my body. I decided I should enjoy myself because it was never happening again. Ever.

"Turn over," Lionel commanded. He took his dick out of me and I turned over and got up on all fours because I knew that was what he wanted. "Damn you have a nice ass," Lionel commented as he entered me again. The second time was all about cumming. Lionel rode me hard and fast. He came first, and I quickly followed.

I had to lower myself on the bed after I came. Lionel stayed on top of me with his softening dick buried in me. I took deep breaths, trying to regain my composure. I kept feeling Lionel's muscles against my back and remembering how much I had missed him. It felt good to have him on top of me. I started to protest when he pulled out of me and rolled on to the other part of the bed. "Thank you," he said out loud. I remained quiet. "Did you hear what I said?" he asked. I turned my face in his direction and looked in his eyes. "I said thank you," he told me.

"You're welcome," I responded without thinking.

"I love you."

I sighed. "I love you, too."

His face lit up and I couldn't stop myself from smiling back at him because seeing him so happy made me feel happy.

"So does this mean we're back together?" he asked with enthusiasm in his voice and happiness in his eyes.

My smile disappeared. Reality returned. "No. I'm not sure what this means, but we're definitely not back together. I can't handle that."

"But I need you. I can't handle being without you. That has to count for something."

"It does. I'm just not sure what." The happiness faded from his eyes and I felt that familiar tingle of joy at causing him pain. "This was my way of saying goodbye to sex with you."

The next thing I knew, my naked body was crashing against the floor. Lionel had kicked me off the bed. He jumped up and was standing over me. I was sure he was going to hit me again, but he didn't. Instead, he put his hand out to help me up. "I'm sorry. I didn't mean to kick you that hard. You have to believe me."

He looked worried. I ignored his outstretched hand and stood up on my own. "You can't play with me like that. Not with the history we have."

"I did it before I thought about it, but I wasn't trying to hurt you."

"I know you weren't."

"Do you mean that?" he asked.

"Yes. I know you weren't trying to hurt me. I can tell the difference."

He stepped towards me and I backed away. "I was just going to hug you."

"Please don't." An awkward silence invaded the room as I started putting on my clothes.

"You don't have to leave."

"Yes I do."

Lionel grabbed his clothes and put them on. We finished dressing at the same time. "I'll walk you to Michael's."

"Okay." I glanced at my old mattress and laughed when I saw the mess we had made.

"What?" Lionel asked.

"We should clean the mattress because that's disgusting. I feel bad for whoever gets that bed."

Lionel laughed. "I missed your sense of humor, too."

"I know, I know. You missed everything about me."

"I did and now that I have you again, I'm never letting you go."

Something in his tone made me shudder on the inside, but I quickly passed it off as my overactive imagination. "You don't have me again," I reminded him.

"I meant as friends. We are at least friends now, right?"

"I guess so."

"Well that's good enough for me, for now."

The walk to Michael's apartment was filled with chatter about random things but we never discussed us. Lionel startled me when he followed me inside the door of Michael's apartment building and gave me a hug and a quick peck in the hallway.

"We're just friends," I said as I pushed him away. He shook his head and said goodbye. I wondered what the hell was wrong with me as I stood and watched him walk down the hallway. He stopped when he reached the door and he turned around and waved. I waved back and I could feel myself smiling, which made me furious. I didn't want to react to him like that. I wanted to be upset with him. I opened the door and walked in Michael's apartment. Troy and Michael were waiting for me. "I don't want to talk about my day," I warned them as I stormed through the room and directly to the bedroom and slammed the door. I listened at the door for a few minutes and heard Troy and Michael talking about Von. They thought I was upset about him. If only they knew.

Chapter 25

Goodbye My Lover

I couldn't bring myself to tell Michael or Troy or Henry about what happened with Lionel. I briefly discussed Von's existence with them and I let them believe that Von was the demon that was haunting me. I didn't go to my classes the rest of the week and I sent all of my teachers an email explaining that I had over-exerted myself on my first day back and I needed a little time to recuperate. My teachers were all understanding, even the teachers I hadn't met seemed sympathetic of my situation. I wondered if all of them knew that my crazy ex-boyfriend accidentally pushed me down a flight of stairs. It felt as if everyone knew.

Friday night, I was sitting in Michael's bedroom, depressed and angry because I kept remembering how it felt to be in Lionel's arms again and I wanted to call him, but at the same time I felt stupid for wanting to have anything to do with him. I didn't want to be like Henry's aunt. I didn't want to die and I didn't want to be smacked around. I didn't want to be insulted or constantly accused of things I didn't do. Lionel couldn't give me what I needed and he was incapable of having the type of relationship I wanted, but my heart looked beyond all of his faults and focused on how he made me feel. I needed Lionel to want me and to need to be with me.

The best thing for both of us was for us to move on and separate, but I wasn't sure how to do it. Having Troy around was a good distraction and for a while I thought he could have been something more but then I realized that I wasn't over Lionel. I said I was and I wished saying it made it true, but it didn't. Lionel had his hooks in me so deep that just seeing him changed everything inside of me and screwed up my circuitry until all I could think about was him. I had to figure out what was going on in my head and why I was making such horrible, ill- advised decisions whenever Lionel was around. I needed to know how I could still want to be with him given our history. There had to be a reason.

There I was, sitting on Michael's bed pretending to read a book but really thinking about Lionel, when the bedroom door swung open. I looked up and saw Troy. Seeing him brought a smile to my face. "Hey Troy."

"When were you going to tell me that you hooked up with Lionel?"

"What are you talking about?"

"Von cornered me after practice. He said that you and Lionel were together on Monday. He said you did it in your old room and then Lionel walked you here."

"I made a mistake."

"So it's true?" I nodded. "Why would you do something like that? I thought you were trying to move on. You can't move on if you refuse to let him go."

"Don't you think I know that? That's why I've been so depressed. I don't want to be with him anymore, but when I'm around him, I can't control how I feel. You have no idea what it's like to know that something is bad for you, but want it anyway." I looked away.

"But you were almost over him."

"I know."

"So what happened?"

"I keep seeing him. I wish I could stop wanting to be with him and I hate myself because I can't, but when I see him everything is different."

"Well hating yourself won't solve your problem but I know what will."

"What?"

Troy walked over and sat next to me. "I know you hate to hear this and I've been trying to stay out of your business with Lionel, but the best thing for both of you is to stay away from each other. I'm sure he doesn't want to hurt you and I'm sure he feels horrible about the things he's done, but nothing he can say or do will ever change what happened and I'm sure you miss your friendship and you want to be near him and only think about the good times, but you can't live like that. You can't pretend that things are fine."

"I don't pretend things are fine. He knows how I feel about us. He knows I won't be with him like that again."

"Does he? Hell, do you? You say one thing and do another. You don't want to be with him like that, but you were anyway, and why? Is he that good in bed?"

"It has nothing to do with sex."

"Then what is it about him that makes you want to be with him even though he likes to hit you?"

"I don't know. I wish I did."

"Well you need to think about it. You guys are toxic together and even you know that's true. He's not good enough for you, but worse, he's not good for you." Troy kissed the side of my head. "You're a good guy, but my God you're so stupid sometimes. You can do better than Lionel." He laughed. "I mean come on. You could have me."

I grinned and looked at him. "I did have you."

"Once. You had me once, but you could have me all the time."

I pushed him away. "Go cook dinner or something."

He stood. "Michael's cooking dinner, but I'll go bother him since you want to be alone. You should go to your classes on Monday. You can't hide from Lionel forever." He left the room and closed the door.

All I wanted to do was let Lionel go and move on with my life but it seemed impossible. Troy was right. I had to get away from Lionel. I couldn't walk around campus with the constant fear of seeing him and the certainty of knowing that I was likely to do something I would regret. I wished Lionel had never followed me to college. Everything would have been different and most likely better for both of us.

I heard a commotion in the apartment and then I heard something crash to the floor. My thoughts had to take a backseat as I went out to see what was going on. I had visions of Troy and Michael fighting, but I was way off. I walked out and saw Von hit Troy in the face.

"That's for pushing me!" Von yelled at him.

I looked around and saw Michael walking from the kitchen with the phone in his hand, "I'm going to call the police if you don't leave."

"Call them! I came to talk to Lucas for a few minutes and I'm not leaving until I talk to him."

"What do you want with me?" I asked.

Von noticed me for the first time. "Lionel is fucked up and it's your fault. How could you toy with his emotions like that? You know what he's been through. You know how screwed up he is! I asked you to call him. I didn't ask you to let him fuck you and then disappear. Why won't you answer your phone when he calls?"

"Wait, wait, I'm still stuck on the fuck you part," Michael said. Michael looked at me. "You were with Lionel?" I nodded my head. "Please tell me it wasn't here. Not in my apartment, just not in my apartment. Tell me you didn't do it in my apartment."

"I didn't. It happened on campus, in our old dorm room. It should have never happened."

"But it did happen and now Lionel is a complete mess. Why won't you talk to him?" Von asked.

"It's only been four days! I needed some space. What's the fucking problem? I told him right after it happened that we were just friends." I was getting angry.

"I know you aren't getting a fucking attitude with me! Not after what you did to my brother. You got him all twisted up and shit. He hasn't eaten anything since he saw you, and that bitch Niqua has been sniffing around. That ho gave him Chlamydia. He doesn't need her, but if you keep fucking with his head, he may end up fucking her. You can't let that shit happen."

"Why not? It's none of my business who he does and does not fuck. I don't care, let Niqua have him. It's probably for the best anyway."

"For the best? You know his track record with her. How could you say it's for the best?"

"He needs to be with someone other than me. I'm not the right person for him. I wish I was, but I'm not."

"But you are. You made him better. He needs you in his life."

"But I don't need him in mine. You can't force me to be with him."

"If you ever loved him, I wouldn't have to force you because you would be there for him. I know he did you wrong when you were together but he is trying to change. He's changing everything about himself just to make your little white ass happy. I'm not asking you to love him again. I'm not asking you to let him fuck you again. I just want you to talk to him and if you can't even talk to him then I hope you rot in hell because you know how Lionel is. You know he's going to do something dumb soon. If he comes after you, don't say I didn't warn you, because I'm here right now telling you that he's not doing well. Give him a week and we'll see if he hasn't managed to get his hands on you by then."

"Is that a threat?"

"No, it's a warning. You're driving him crazy. He's getting upset and obsessive and I'm afraid of what he might do to himself and to you if you don't talk to him soon. I mean best case scenario is he fucks Niqua and moves on, but I have a feeling it's bigger than that. If you keep toying with him, he's going to bite back hard. He wanted to come here tonight but I told him I would come instead. I came because I was afraid of what he was going to do."

"He was going to hurt me?"

"It wouldn't be the first time, now would it?" Von asked with malice in his voice.

"Shut up Von!" Troy shouted.

"Oh are you going to jump me like you did Lionel? He told me all about you guys. You, Henry and Michael: a bunch of punks. You didn't even face him man-to-man, but I'm standing here right now. Take a swing, motherfucker! Come on, I dare you. Hit me! Come on, hit me!"

I walked in front of Von. "Calm down. You told me what you needed to tell me, now leave." It took a few minutes but I finally convinced Von to leave. I slammed the door and turned on Michael and Troy. "You guys beat up Lionel?" I asked in disbelief. Troy and

Michael didn't say anything. Their faces admitted their guilt. "I can't believe you guys."

"He deserved it," Michael told me.

"He deserves a lot of things, but that's not one of them," I said.

"He needed to know how it felt to be knocked around."

"Michael what the fuck do you think is Lionel's problem? He's been knocked around all his life! That's why he was so violent with me. My relationship with him has nothing to do with either of you. If I take him back, that's on me."

"You're not planning on taking him back are you?" Michael asked.

"And what if I am? The therapy seems to be helping him a lot. He's not as violent as he used to be."

"That's because we beat the hell out of him," Michael screamed.

I left the two of them in the living room and I went to the bedroom to gather my thoughts. I took a nap and Henry came in and woke me up so I could eat. The way he tried to baby me, let me know that Troy and Michael had filled him in on the day's events, but he didn't ask me any questions, he just opened his mouth and said, "I'm sorry about what we did to Lionel."

"You should be."

I was unable to eat anything, so I sat at the table and stared at my plate while I thought about Lionel being beaten by my friends. I finally reached a point where I had to say something, "What you guys did was wrong. I know why you did it, but it was still wrong." I excused myself from the table and went back to Michael's room to hibernate.

I was a wreck on Monday morning. My stomach performed a variety of gymnastic routines as I walked to campus with Michael and Troy, who had not said much since I forgave them the night before. We said goodbye and I promised to meet up with Michael after my class.

I went in class and was pleased not to see Von. The class dragged on but I was grateful because the longer the class felt, the more prepared I was to face the people on campus again. Class ended and I walked out the door.

My nose was ambushed by a foul smell. I turned my head in the direction of the stench and saw Lionel. My body was instantly paralyzed. The person behind me bumped in to me. Lionel grabbed my arm and jerked me to the side. "We need to talk," he growled.

"How did you know what room I was in?" I looked at him and he was a mess. His condition reminded me of the bus ride, but he wasn't disheveled this time, he was drunk. He reeked of alcohol and funk. I figured he started drinking Friday night and didn't stop until he decided to come track me down. It was too early in the morning to be drunk.

"Von told me where to find you." He pulled my arm and led me down the hallway towards the back staircase.

"Let me go." I tried to get away but I couldn't because his grip was too strong. "Where are you taking me?"

"Away from them."

"From who?"

"From them. They're turning you against me and I won't have it. I'm sick of playing nice with them. They have no right to fill your head with all that nonsense. Why can't we be friends? I gave up everything to be with you. I could have played ball for a college that was ranked in the top five in the nation, but I gave it up to be here and I'm not going to let you go. I just need to get you away from them so you can see that they're bad for you. They want you to hate me. We were great until they started dipping in our business."

Lionel sounded like someone who had slipped over the edge. "You do realize you sound crazy don't you?"

"Shut up."

"What are you going to do, walk me through campus like this?"

"Yes and you're going to keep your mouth shut."

"Why?"

"Because you owe me that much."

He walked me down the stairs. There were only a few students using the backstairs and none of them paid us any attention. I should have screamed for help but I didn't. I let Lionel lead me down the stairs and outside. We must have walked past a hundred people on our way to our old dorm room and I never cried out for help. His grip on my arm was tight, but he wasn't stopping me from speaking. I had to admit to myself that I wanted him to take me away. I wanted to be alone with him because being alone with him excited me. It was always a little scary and I was always on edge, but something about the way it made me feel and the rush of not knowing what he might do from one second to the next, something about that was indescribably appealing. Every nerve in my body was charged when he was around. When he was close to me there was so much going on inside of me, so many emotions pulling me in different directions, that I thought I could spontaneously combust and burn for days. I hated and loved him at the same time.

I wondered what he was planning as he opened the room door. "I bet they'll never think to look for us here," I said, hoping to get a rise out of him.

He shoved me in the room. "Shut up."

"Or what?" He closed the door and grabbed me from behind. He didn't hit me and that impressed me because it meant he was really changing.

He led me towards my bed while he kissed the back of my neck. "I waited for you," he whispered. "I waited for you to get out of the hospital and come back to me and when you didn't, I came to you. I came to you and you rejected me and I let you. I wanted to give you your space but it was eating me up inside that you wouldn't even let me be your friend. It was hell while you were in the hospital, but that can't compare to this." His hand grabbed the back of my head and forced me to look at the bed. I closed my eyes. "Open your eyes and look at it! Look at it dammit!" I opened my eyes and saw our old room, still empty and void of all traces of us, besides the stain on my mattress. Lionel guided me to my knees. He pushed my face so close to the stain that I felt cross eyed as I looked at the spot. "Is that all I mean to you now? Just sex?"

"I'm sorry. It was a mistake. It shouldn't have happened."

"You're just like her!" he shouted. "You're just like her!"

The hairs on the back of my neck stood up. I had spent a week agonizing over having sex with him, but I never thought about how it might have affected him. Von tried to tell me but I was more concerned with my own safety. I knew Lionel's past. How could I do that to him? How could I have sex with him and toss him aside like he was nothing? What happened was wrong. I should have been stronger. I could have made enough noise for someone to notice and come see what was going on, but I let Lionel keep me in the room.

I was as guilty as he was. I knew what he wanted from me and I played my part and let him be the aggressor.

I wasn't like her though. She loved a part of him, but I loved all of him. Everything clicked in to place and I realized how true my thoughts were. I loved all of him and that's why I couldn't completely let him go. I wanted to fix him. I had to let Lionel know that I wasn't just using him. "I'm sorry. I wasn't trying to use you. You're more to me than sex. You know that. You have to know that! I'm not like her. I love you."

I expected him to go on a tirade about how I couldn't love him because if I did I would be with him, but he didn't. In a very quiet voice he asked, "After everything I've done, how can you still love me?"

"I know who you really are." I felt him move from behind me and I turned to my right and saw him beside me. I looked him square in his eyes and said, "I know who you really are and I have hope that you'll find that person again. This isn't you Lionel. I don't know who it is. I don't know if it's your father or if it's her, but I know it's not you."

"Don't you get it? I am them. They made me."

"You don't have to be them. You're better than that."

I saw the tears building in his eyes. "What if I'm not?"

"I know you are."

"I hurt you," he commented.

"I know."

"I'm sorry."

"I know." I wanted to add, 'you always are,' but the time was wrong for smart comments.

The tears in his eyes began to escape and slide down his face. "I'm scared."

"Of what?"

"That I'll always be like this."

I put my arms around him. "You're going to finish getting help and you'll be fine. I know you will. And you want to know something else?"

"What?"

"When you finish getting help I'll be here waiting for you, as your friend."

"You will?"

"I promise I will, but you have to get help and you have to finish your program and stop drinking. I can't be friends with you if you stay like this and if you ever hit me again, I'll be done with you forever."

"I'll do whatever you want me to do, but you're going to have to help me. I can't do it without you."

"You can call me and we can talk on the phone. Other than that, I don't think we should have much contact with each other until you get the help you need. I'm going to get some help too."

"For what? There's nothing wrong with you."

"Yes there is. I should have never let you treat me the way you did and I need help pinpointing why I can't let you go because it's not normal. If we're going to promise to try to salvage something between us, we both need to be healthy so we don't fall in to the same routine."

I could tell by the way his eyes were watching my lips that he wasn't really listening to me anymore. "Can I kiss you goodbye?" he asked.

"I don't think that's a good idea."

"Just a little kiss."

I gave him a peck on his cheek then I stood up and backed towards the door. "I need to leave now, but you call me if you need to talk, okay?"

"Okay." I had the door open when I heard him say my name, "Lucas."

I looked at him, "Yes."

"Do you think we'll ever be more than friends again?"

I smiled. "Who knows?" I closed the door and left him alone in the room. I walked out the building and took about three steps before someone shouted, "Lucas!"

I spotted Michael running towards me. "Where the hell have you been? I was looking all over for you."

"And you didn't think to check my dorm room?"

"I figured you wouldn't go there after what happened with you and Lionel last week."

"Well you were wrong."

"Why didn't you wait for me? I would have walked over here with you?"

"I needed to do this on my own."

"Do what?"

"Figure out who I am to Lionel and who he is to me."

"And?"

"I figured out that he was as mean to me as I let him be and I have to take some responsibility for what happened between us. The first time was completely his fault, but I knew what to expect the other times and I didn't leave. I can't blame him for all of it when I know part of it was me. I was supposed to be Lionel's savior. He wanted me to save him from himself and I let him down, but I get it now and I'm ready to help him the best way I can."

"And how's that?"

"By supporting him and giving him some space to get professional help because I can't fix him. Nobody can fix him. He can get better though. And as far as who he is to me, I think that's still a work in progress."

About the Author

LT writes stories from the comfort of Ohio. LT Ville has no children. LT is an internet author who enjoys writing poetry and stories that focus on the lives and actions of gay individuals.